WHAT OTHERS ARE SAYING

Ben Zama's book is a compelling blend of romance, superstition, and the devastating reality of the health-care debacle that still exists in Cameroon. I can attest to the dilemma of undiagnosed diabetes in Cameroon having participated in several medical mission trips to Cameroon. Worthy to mention is the fact that as a medical practitioner in the US, I see undiagnosed diabetes as a plight in America too as 27.8 percent of those with diabetes in the US are reported undiagnosed. What more of Cameroon? Thank God for Ben Zama's courage and insight as he puts words to what is the truth with clarity and precision. *Mama Sango* also peers with humor into areas of cultural and social disconnect faced by Cameroonians who return home after staying in countries such as America for too long.

—Liza Ekole, PharmD., PhD
VP of Fountain of Hope Missions
Professional Health-Care Coach

Mama Sango is an enthralling novel that should be shown to all. Ben Zama's heartfelt journey through Mama Sango's life will open many eyes to the medical issues that plague areas of the developing world. The cultural experience will shock and awe, while leaving readers wanting to make a contribution to the movement this story presents. Mama Sango's tale is surely one that will impact many lives and will bring about a sense of humility when examining one's own life.

—Jarred Barch
Technology Leadership Program

After sharing his diabetes diagnosis with his friend, Mr. Charm, the author learns about Mama Sango, who died from undiagnosed diabetes. This presents him with an opportunity to delve into the life of Mama Sango. Mama Sango's daily experiences as an ordinary Cameroonian woman are depicted. Her story brings to light some of the practices and customs of the Bamenda (Abakwa) people. Part of the book is about Marie Noel, a bushfaller and Mama Sango's sister. Her life is intriguing, to say the least. When Marie Noel learns that Mama Sango's death was the result of undiagnosed diabetes, she uses her funeral for diabetes awareness.

The book is interspersed with lingo familiar to Cameroonians, which makes the messages vivid and impactful. It is full of suspense and leaves you yearning for part 2.

—Cecilia Zama
M.Ed, Educator, Fairfax County Public Schools

Zama's artfully crafted story highlights the need for education around the world on the detection, prevention, and care for the diabetic condition. In addition to education, however, the importance of a greater connection between cultures is relevant as well. Bridging the expansive distance between Cameroon and the US, this heartfelt tale helps readers to connect with the characters and to develop an appreciation and respect for the rich stories, heritage, beliefs, struggles, and triumphs of the people of Cameroon. I learned something of the culture in Cameroon, while being swept away with the story of Mama Sango.

—Katie Scanlan
Author of *Iceland: A "Type A" Travel Adventures Guide*

for chop, matu, siri, sajah, nji, and aghanwi

MAMA SANGO

"The world belongs to those who study."

—*A.C. Zama*
(1907–1982)

MAMA SANGO

The tragic, untimely, unnecessary and preventable
death of a hard-working mother

BENJAMIN ZAMA

TATE PUBLISHING
AND ENTERPRISES, LLC

Published by Tate Publishing & Enterprises, LLC
127 E. Trade Center Terrace | Mustang, Oklahoma 73064 USA
1.888.361.9473 | www.tatepublishing.com

Tate Publishing is committed to excellence in the publishing industry. The company reflects the philosophy established by the founders, based on Psalm 68:11,
"The Lord gave the word and great was the company of those who published it."

Book design copyright © 2016 by Tate Publishing, LLC. All rights reserved.
Cover design by Samson Lim
Interior design by Jake Muelle

Published in the United States of America

ISBN: 978-1-68270-870-5
Fiction / African American / General
16.06.10

"I had no shoes and complained,
until I met a man who had no feet."

—Indian Proverb

CONTENTS

FOREWORD

Mama Sango is a captivating story that once started, you are eager to continue to find out what is ahead. A story intertwined with love, childbearing, and health, *Mama Sango* is a lived experience story that as you read along, it becomes difficult not to relate or feel connected to some of its content.

As a health-care provider, I particularly empathize with Mama Sango's negative outcome. As I read her story and struggles to deal with diabetes as she ran a business that fed a community, I found myself subconsciously teaching her as she had complaints of polyuria and polydipsia throughout. It also felt real to me as I read on the cultural and modern medical care disputes that took place after Mama Sango's unpleasant experience at the hospital.

We are in a society where proper education and training of future health-care providers is very crucial. Continuous education and refresher courses for health-care practitioners cannot be emphasized enough. Well-trained practitioners who are constantly at the frontline of health-care facilities are highly needed as they are the ones to educate, enlighten, and promote the health of its community members. I strongly believe education is key, and prevention is better than cure.

It will not be far-fetched if I say that as adults in society, we are also patients. The difference amongst us is that some people know their health status (patients) and can better abide to behaviors, attitudes, and practices that will promote positive health outcomes. On the other hand, there are those individuals who are not aware of their health history (nonpatients they claim) but are walking around with major medical problems that usually lead to negative health outcomes such as heart attacks and strokes.

As you read along, ask yourself; what can I deduce from this story? How can I use this story to better my health as a so-called patient or nonpatient? And finally, if you are in the health-care industry, ask yourself how you can better your practice as a practitioner to help save lives, irrespective of your geographic region as health care is and should be a global effort? Without further ado, I urge you to read on and find out for yourselves.

—Dr. Fonya Atabong, RN, DNP

1

THE REASONING

On February 14, 2014, I arrived at the Primary Care Clinic on Greenville Road in Dallas for a checkup, after an eight-hour glucose fast. As I thumbed through the pages of *Inc. Magazine* waiting for my blood test results, the doctor—a young Indian lady with a serious look on her face and papers in hand—called my name and asked me to follow her.

As we both took our seats in the exam room, she exhaled and with a stern look, declared, "You are a walking dead man. Your blood sugar is almost 300 and your A1C is 13.5. That is way too high, and I'm surprised you are walking in here like you are King Kong. No more rice, no more potatoes, no more starches, no more white anything, no more, no more…"

If not for the seriousness with which she addressed the situation, I would have laughed at the seemingly comic melodic rise and fall of her accent, as she rattled off the dos and don'ts. The effect was more numbing to me, because I had no clue of what she was talking about. I felt dejected. I spent the rest of the day in bed, unable to function.

"It could be worse," said my dear friend, Mr. Fred Cham, after I shared my malaise the next day. "Many people die from this disease back at home without being aware of it. There are stories of diabetics going to the hospital and being infused with glucose, and because they don't know that they are sick, they don't object to these infusions, and the results are catastrophic. Do you remember my cousin, Mama Sango? At least you know what you have and how you can control it." After this conversation, it occurred to me that I had little to complain about, for I was fortunate to be in the United States of America where medical facilities are the best in the world. I had all the information I could possibly want at my fingertips, and yet complained about being diabetic. In effect, I was complaining of not having shoes, when there were people who were without feet!

As soon as Mr. Cham finished narrating the story about his cousin, my curiosity got the best of me. I pried some more into her life and wondered how many people had died as a result of this negligence. More importantly, how many more would die because of ignorance?

The ensuing story is that of an ordinary, hard-working woman, who carried out her normal daily routine on that fateful day, unaware of how tragic the day would end. Mama Sango's story illustrates the different outcomes that can result from an awareness surrounding this terminal disease—or the lack thereof.

2

MAMA SANGO

The day started uneventfully. Mama Sango stirred as the cock crowed. There was no need for an alarm clock. For years, the roosters in Abakwa kept her on track, as if they understood the need for her to be up around 5:00 a.m. every day.

Her body ached. She wished it were Saturday. How she treasured those extra hours in bed! Pa Sango snored gently beside her on the other side of the bed—the bed they had shared since the day she moved in. How distant yesterday's memories seemed. They used to sleep like a knot, woven to each other. Now they slept on each side of the bed, except on those rare nights when unexplained desires gripped either of them, enough to be entangled again.

She forced herself up, the routine of the day firmly installed in her brain. She felt dizzy. She hadn't been feeling well these past couple of days. Without brushing her teeth, she gulped down a large glass of water to quench the thirst that had been frequent these past few days. She had been drinking a lot of water and urinating a lot. She made a mental note to go to the hospital that afternoon.

She tiptoed into Sango's room, close enough to hear him breathing, and stood for a moment, as the memories of his birth took over her thoughts. She smiled, raised her eyes to the ceiling (her way of saying thank you to the One above), and walked out.

She squinted, as the harsh light lit the kitchen. On the stove sat the beans she had soaked the night before. Thankfully, Pa Sango remembered to buy cooking gas yesterday when deliveries came in. Gas supply never used to be a problem, until the ghost town demonstrations that engulfed Abakwa. For a moment, images of the protests flashed through her mind. There she was, on the front lines, hurling tomatoes and green peppers at the tax collectors who had been harassing the traders on a daily basis. Soon, passersby joined in, and before the night was over, Abakwa was in turmoil. The demonstrations, organic in nature, were spontaneous at first, and then gradually morphed into an organized political resistance. The English-speaking population had grown weary of being marginalized and sought to deprive the government of revenue by shutting down businesses and services. The government responded with lethal force and employed other tactics, including the rationing of commodities. Electricity, water, and gas were weapons of choice. The availability of gas was now sporadic, as the government collectively punished everyone in Abakwa for their audacity to rise up against it. She turned on the gas cooker. Blue flames shot up with the clicking of the igniter. She slowly adjusted the burner to the highest flame setting, satisfied that the beans will be cooked in about an hour.

It was still dark outside. The pressure on her bladder was excruciating, making it difficult for her to cover the distance between the house and the latrine. Halfway to the latrine, she gingerly stepped into the brush and lifted her kaba, barely having enough time to pull down her underwear as nature's tap gushed out, splashing warm fluid around her ankles. She subconsciously thanked whoever designed the *kaba*, the free-flowing versatile gown that goes with any occasion or activity.

* * *

Mama Sango didn't need to measure the flour. She had done this countless times, and by now, her intuition and sight were enough. She poured exact amounts of salt, sugar, and water into a bowl with no calibrations! As she mixed the ingredients in the bowl, she was startled by the presence of a shadow by her side. Sango was standing next to her, rubbing his eyes and looking visibly disoriented.

"Why are you up so early?" she asked. Then she noticed she had left the door to his room ajar, letting in light from the kitchen. "Do you have to pee-pee?" He shook his head.

"Then go back to bed," she said, leading him back to his bedroom.

3

THE SEARCH

Sango had been difficult to come by. She remembered her struggles trying to conceive; the fertility clinics, the "prophets," the traditional doctors, and the insults and humiliation at the hands of her in-laws when conception eluded her. The taunts were scathing, especially from the women less-endowed in the beauty department. She became the topic of conversations.

"See that one. She fried her belly thinking she'd remain young forever," said Mama Clara, Pa Sango's cousin.

"She's getting punished for all the abortions she committed," enjoined Mama Sisia, Mama Clara's friend and fellow small-food vendor.

"What are you doing here, useless woman? Just eating my brother's money for nothing," commented Aunt Mangwi, as she threw out Mama Sango's belongings on the street. Pa Sango was not amused when he got home that evening. This act, he considered, was a personal affront. Being action-oriented, Pa Sango could not contain the rage that burned in him and thus, didn't have the patience to wait for a taxi. He took long strides to traverse the mile or so distance that separated his residence from that of his sister's in a very short time. He lumbered into Pa Asongwe's residence unannounced, veins taut on his forehead. Aunt Mangwi was startled and frozen in place by the look on her brother's face. With lightening speed, he picked up his sister by the shoulders like a rag doll and slammed her against the wall, with her feet dangling about two feet in the air.

"Don't you ever, ever, ever disrespect my wife again."

After what seemed like an eternity to Aunt Mangwi, he set her down and calmly walked out. The taunts from Aunt Mangwi's inner circle stopped as soon as the news spread; not so from the distant relatives.

Mama Sango endured the torture, sometimes crying herself to sleep. The most comforting thing was that Pa Sango stood by her. He truly loved her and rebuffed calls from his family to divorce her. Though he would have loved to hold a child of his own in his arms; come what may, he had decided to stick with Mama Sango. She was the love of his life, the only woman who loved him for who he was. She stood by him when he was down and almost out. His thriving supply business had failed. He supported the wrong political party, and all the contracts dried up. He reminisced about the good old days when the money flowed. The cars, the women, chicken parlors, friends galore, and all the glamour! Suddenly, his world stopped turning. His friends disappeared! Cars broke down, and there was no money to fix or fuel them. The girls vanished, and Pa Sango could not crawl out of his bed for days. And then it happened!

Mama Sango, a former small food supplier of his, came knocking, curious to find out why he hadn't been buying her produce anymore. "*Massa* money, *massa* Money!" She banged on the bedroom window, having determined that he was home and not answering the front door. Her persistence paid off. She took one look at him and instinctively understood.

"What are you doing in bed at one in the afternoon?" she asked, Then she ordered, "You need to shave,"

He thought, *Who the heck does she think she is ordering him around?*

* * *

There was no running water. Abakwa had gone without running water for the past three days. She looked around the kitchen, grabbed a bucket, and walked the one hundred or so yards to fetch him some water.

Some sweet aroma wafted out into the yard, as he approached the house from having his shower outside. He was astonished. She had taken over the kitchen as if she lived and belonged there. He stood there in the middle of the kitchen with a towel around his waist and suddenly became aware of the uncontrollable bulge midway down his stout frame. Mama Sango winced at the enormous sight. Embarrassed, he turned around and hurriedly walked into his room.

She tiptoed in, threw her kaba on the floor, and planted her firm round breast on his back. An irresistible surge of energy shot through him. He spun around, pulled her to him, and squeezed her so tight she could hardly breathe. Without a word, they were entangled in bliss.

From that moment, they became inseparable. The change in Pa Sango's aura was unmistakable. The swagger for which he was known for by eligible and not-so-eligible women returned. Some, who had shunned him just a few months ago, began smiling at him more often and seeking his attention. Pa Sango hardly noticed, for all his attention was focused on his new *flame*—a flame that unlike most had stayed burning. Gone were those days when his flames fizzled before the cock crowed. Mama Sango was the missing link he had been searching for—or was she? He was not in the business of reliving the past. He was determined to enjoy the manna that God had literally dropped in his lap, the manna he had conveniently discounted during his heyday.

Pa Sango became a constant presence at Mama Sango's food stall. Her colleagues were flabbergasted at the improbable union. The fact that Pa Sango, a high-society socialite, could stoop so low as to date a fellow trader was a hopeful reminder that nothing was impossible. For three months, they dated. His mother did not find it amusing that her upper-middle-class-socialite son, was dating a commoner—a mere street food vendor! He was saddened by the fact that his own mother did not attend his wedding. His family's reception was cold, but he was oblivious to them. He would do anything to please her. Having a baby was her top priority, and he was by her side all the way.

The first three years had been frustrating. She timed her periods, exercised, ate the right foods, and did all they were advised to do to no avail. The frightening thought of never having a baby was beginning to take root. Then she listened to a song, "Louer Dieu." The lyrics reminded her of Sarah in the Bible, who remained faithful to God and conceived at eighty years old!

They visited all the "men of God" who claimed to have the power to bless her womb and make her fruitful. Prophet Doright, one of the most sought after "man of God," prayed for both of them for three consecutive weeks. The last week of the scheduled four-week prayer session was to be a *special prayer session* only for Mama Sango. As part of the preparation, the session was timed so that Mama Sango would be in ovulation. She was to eat specifically selected fruits and foods chosen by the Prophet. She was to sleep a minimum of seven hours every night for the next seven days. Prayer sessions were to start at seven and lasted for seven hours.

Mama Sango dutifully went through all the preparatory steps in readiness to receive a miracle baby. She arrived at the prayer house half an hour early. Prophet Doright was in the sanctuary, getting holy. He continued his rituals, paying no attention to Mama Sango. After what seemed like an eternity, he rose up from where he was kneeling and motioned for Mama Sango to kneel down closer to him. He led the prayer, invoking God with incantations—some intelligible, and some not. He held her hands, raised them up to the ceiling, imploring the Almighty to intervene. He prayed for Prophet Elijah to intercede, to touch the barren womb, and to make it bear fruit.

Two hours of serious prayer elapsed, and it was now time to proceed to the "holy room," where all the miracles of the other women had been granted. The room was dimly lit, with a mixture of red, blue, and yellow halogen lights. It gave the ambiance of a smooth jazzy nightclub. To the right was a queen-size bed, exquisitely draped with golden tassels hanging from the flowery covers. The pillow cases matched the bed cover and the pillows were carefully placed to slightly lean on the headboard, exposing about a ten-inch sheet of satin-colored silk. A red sheet covered the wall over the headboard, with a golden cross in the middle. On the bedside table were a standing crucifix, a large red

Bible, and a boom box. To the left was a small mahogany table with two plush chairs and a vase full of roses. By the table was a recessed wooden case with a silver communion cup, two plates, two wine glasses, and a bottle of clear half-filled liquid. Further down past the table was a door heading into the bathroom.

Mama Sango quickly made a mental note of the room, remembering her dad's advice, "When you get to a new house, note where all the escape routes are. It could save your life."

"Please have a seat," he said.

Mama Sango sat in the chair closest to the door.

"Before we start, you need to drink this," the Prophet said, as he poured out half a glass of the clear liquid from the bottle before handing it to Mama Sango.

"Can I throw out my gum in the bathroom?"

"Sure."

She poured out the substance in the sink, rinsed the glass, and carefully filled it with water to the same level. She then gulped the water down, in full view of the prophet.

"At this point, I'd like to ask you to please take off your clothes and lie on the bed, facing up. Leave on your brazier and underwear," he said.

"Praise be to God Almighty, amen," the prophet began.

"In the name of Jesus, amen.

"Our heavenly Father, glory be thy name, fill this room with your spirit. Come down and touch this barren womb and make it fertile again, as you have always done. May your will be done, oh Jesus of Nazareth. I submit to you, oh Lord, to bless these hands through which your blessings will flow. I call upon you, oh Lord, to cast away all the evil spirits that have prevented this womb from bearing fruit, that no weapon formed against her will prosper. Cover her with your blood that today be the day she has been waiting for. Show your mercy, oh Lord. I ask for your favor and your anointing that through me, your blessings will flow into her, oh Lord, and that this day be the day you have chosen to shame the devil and show the world how great you are. In Jesus's name I pray, amen."

Why is she still alert? He wondered.

"Now we are getting to the final phase, and I am going to prepare you to receive the miracle. You are going to be exorcised, and I ask that you do as I say."

Mama Sango's mind was in a race against itself. She felt like her heart was going to jump out of her body. She employed all the yoga techniques she'd heard about to stay calm.

The prophet moved closer to the bed, leaned over, and pressed the play button on the boom box. The music was esoteric and enchanting. Ocean waves could be heard rising and falling, birds chirping in unison as if choreographed, a lone violin played in the distance, and piano riffs embellished the intricately arranged chord progressions. It was the kind of music played in massage therapy booths for relaxation.

Mama Sango appeared relaxed, though apprehensive, but was determined to go to the sweet or bitter end. *Nothing good comes easy*, she told herself, and she had come too far to turn back now.

"In Jesus's name, amen," said the prophet. "*Ababa ramkurusami ishika bababa lami.*"

For a while, the prophet rambled on loudly at first, with his hands pulling something invisible out of the air above and motioning it toward Mama Sango's stomach, and then softly and slowly, as if whispering. Mama Sango pretended to be asleep but watched everything through half-closed eyes.

The Prophet continued his rituals, progressing from speaking softly to uttering guttural sounds. His hands now descended from flailing in the air to gently caressing her stomach. He bid his time, believing that his concoction was taking effect. His caresses were progressively sensual, with the tips of his fingers gently coming in contact with her skin in outwardly circular motions. He went from the top of her belly button down to the tip of her underwear; each time, gradually inching his way down to her groin area. His breathing became labored, and Mama Sango could see his eyes were closed and his face toward the ceiling. With his left hand still caressing her, he lifted the frock over his head with the right hand to reveal nothing underneath but a fully erect penis.

Mama Sango knew she had to act. She knew she had to be careful, because one wrong move and she could be dead.

Prophet Doright was now naked. He kneeled between Mama Sango's legs and gently grabbed them by the ankles, slowly lifting them up in an effort to slide down her underwear.

Mama Sango saw an opportunity. She let him lift her legs all the way up, and with all the strength she could muster, kicked the prophet in the groin.

"*Aaaiiieee*," moaned the prophet and fell out of the bed, prostrating in pain.

Mama Sango jumped out of the bed, grabbed the bottle with the clear liquid, and smashed it on the prophet's head before making her getaway.

That was the last time anybody in Abakwa saw or heard from prophet Doright.

4

THE SEARCH CONTINUES

It was five minutes to midnight. The cemetery was eerily quiet. The moon was full, bright, and dead center against the backdrop of a dark-blue sky. Mama Sango paused and looked up to admire the serene beauty. In her revelry, she could hear her father's voice.

"You see the man up there with an axe?" he said, pointing to the moon. "That's Stonghead."

Stronghead's mother, so the story goes, had asked him to fetch wood and water after school. He disobeyed and went to play with his friends. It was dark when his mother came home from a hard day's work at the farm. There was no water to cook or bathe. She was tired, hungry, and very angry. Though it was late into the night, she made Stronghead do his chores. The moon was barely waking up from sleep, as he walked the quarter mile to fetch water. His heart was beating so hard it felt like footsteps beside him. Crickets chirped, owls hooted, and all his mind's eye could see were ghosts waiting in the bushes to pounce on their prey. How relieved he was when he made it back to the house. But the relief was short-lived. His mother asked him to go fetch the wood.

The moon was up but not fully awake and was not amused when Stronghead started splitting wood. He flew down, and in one clean sweep, scooped Stronghead, his axe, and the wood up to the sky. He has been splitting wood on the moon ever since.

"And that's what happens to kids who don' t listen to their parents," she remembered her father saying.

"What's the matter with you?" muttered Pa Sango, nudging her along. She woke up from her trance. Mallam Aladji, the medicine man who was leading them, was a little further down, deep into the cemetery. He crouched, digging a hole beside a chosen grave with a wooden stick between his lips. The cock he brought lay beside him in a cage. He motioned to Pa and Mama Sango to come close. He brought out the cock from the cage and bade both of them to place each of their hands on it. Chanting, he invoked the spirits of their ancestors. He opened the cock's mouth, inserted a wild *alakata* pepper, and then circled the grave seven times with the cock in his hands. After the seventh time, he placed it in the hole he had just dug. If the cock got out and walked away within the hour, the curse placed on Pa Sango of never hearing the sound of a baby's cry by an ex-girlfriend would have been broken. However, if it stayed there for more than an hour, he was out of luck.

They all stood there in the graveyard, quiet, pensive, and apprehensive. In the distance they could hear the frogs croaking and a lone owl hooting. The moon had started its descent to the west, casting short shadows of the late night grave visitors. Mallam Aladji furtively glanced at Pa Sango, genuinely unsure of the unexpected. The cock stood steady with an occasional tilt of the head to the left and then to the right, stretching its neck in the process. A gentle breeze rattled the leaves at the top of trees, swaying back and forth, as if in agreement with the happenings below. The serenity of the surroundings was surreal. Mama Sango saw moving figures—or so she thought. The hairs on the back of her neck stood up. She clutched tightly to Pa Sango's arm, digging her finger nails into his flesh, oblivious to the pain she was inflicting.

About forty-five minutes later, the cock stirred, croaked a bit, tilted its head to the right, and flapped its wings. It jumped out of the hole and made a growling sound as if daring whatever spirits it was confronting to *make its day*. It took deliberate, calculated steps away from the humans, growling all the time. It zigzagged between graves with its stretched neck, propelling it forward with each step and gradually disappeared into the moonlit night. Malam Aladji breathed a sigh of relief. He stretched out his left hand toward Pa Sango, opening his palm and motioning Pa Sango to deposit ten francs, the agreed amount for the ritual. Malam Aladji threw the coin in the hole and scraped the dirt with his feet, burying it in the process.

* * *

Dr. Hope was the most sought-after fertility doctor in Abakwa and its environs. His brain child, Hope Clinic gave thousands of men and women reasons to smile again, sometimes after decades of fruitless forays into elusive child-bearing fantasies. Hope Clinic stood on a hill overlooking the hustle and bustle of Abakwa. Shimmering lights around the perimeter transformed the clinic and its surroundings into a safe haven at night, making it a favorite spot for young lovers. The sheer number of them patrolling the area made it unnecessary for security guards.

In the mornings, throngs of women—and sometimes, grudging men accompanying their wives—lined the hallways patiently waiting to be seen. Dr. Hope, a young, charismatic, and good-looking doctor, had returned home to start his practice, despite lucrative opportunities in America. The enormity of the pain his aunt endured as a barren wife propelled him into this line of work, determined to help as many families as possible. Women from those families disproportionately sought him out, needing his expertise.

Mama Sango was one of them. She was dutiful and mindful of the second-class status she had been subjugated to by her husband's family. It didn't matter that Pa Sango—who was childless at thirty-five, uncommon for a man of his good looks—could be the culprit. The fact that he had been married to a woman for five long years without a child left no room for doubt. The anguish in Mama Sango's countenance sapped any reluctance he had about visiting the fertility clinic together.

Dr. Hope listened with compassion. Listening to Mama Sango made him relive his aunt's anguish. He was determined to help them, despite their economic challenges. Several tests revealed Pa Sango's low sperm count. Pa Sango adhered to Dr. Hope's regimen, in conjunction with prayer vigils and occasional visits to traditional doctors. Six months later, the hopeful but unexpected news was delivered. Dr. Hope's office was a chaotic mess with papers strewn all over the floor, as an excited Mama Sango overturned paper trays. She cried out loudly to God and then gently sobbed as she prostrated in the corner of the doctor's office. Dr. Hope helped her up to a chair. In that instant, an uncontrollable desire swept through her. She looked longingly in his eyes, prepared to give all of herself in appreciation for the life-changing gift he had just made possible. Dr. Hope smiled knowingly, as he recognized the all-too-frequent *look* on his patients' face in their most vulnerable states.

Pa Sango was beyond excitement. Mama Sango glowed as she sat speechless, smiling on the ride home all the way from the clinic. The lovemaking that afternoon was different. It was tender, gentle, and sensual. Mama Sango was a *woman* at last! They were just happy that Sango came along, and did not care about which doctor or pastor deserved the credit.

5

THE ROUTINE

The sun's rays pierced through the haze like laser beams. The sun itself hid behind the clouds, either afraid or ashamed to confront the man-made clouds that emanated from the European diesel-smoke-spewing cars that littered the Abakwa landscape. The haze blanketed Abakwa, which was shaped like an inverted plateau, making it inconvenient for the wind to blow the dense haze away. Rain was the only relief that made it possible for the suffering public to breathe clean air. The pollution was problematic, the population indifferent, and the government oblivious to the fact that it was breeding a new generation of asthmatics.

Mama Sango was too busy with her morning routine to notice or care. It was 7:00 a.m., and the puff-puff mixture she prepared two hours earlier was ready for frying. Over the years, Mama Sango had perfected the art of making this delicacy; the soft, spongy, deep-fried spherical snack made from mixing flour, yeast, water, and sugar. She was running late. Timing was crucial because as was customary, her customers would start showing up in about thirty minutes. The fire from the fire pot was brimming hot, and

Mama Sango sat down in her office—the thatched, wall-less shed—and began the frying process.

Sango was getting ready for school, neatly dressed in his blue shorts and white tucked-in shirt. His black cotton socks—the ones his favorite aunt sent from America—were pulled midway between his ankles and calf. His black leather shoes were different from any other in the whole school, which made him the envy of his classmates.

"Sango," his mother called from the entrance. 'Hurry up!" She dished out two spoonfuls of beans and three puff-puffs for him. He was always the first to taste his mother's beans and puff-puff. She watched as he carried the plate of food into the house. He emerged moments later, ready for school with Pa Sango closely behind. Pa Sango paused for a moment, made small talk, and kissed her on the cheek, and proceeded to accompany Sango to school. She smiled with pride as she watched them, hand in hand fading into the distance.

* * *

The students started trickling in, stopping to buy Mama Sango's specialty. A long orderly line soon formed with youngsters patiently awaiting their turn to be served, a strange sight in a very chaotic country.

"Puff-puff for fifty and beans for fifty" was the student's favorite line. Mama Sango navigated the process with dexterity, multitasking and dishing out the beans and puff-puff while attending to the frying pan. Enough trust had developed between her and her young customers that they deposited and dispensed their own change from a small jar that stood beside her. Sometimes, the jar would fill up, and she would delegate one of the youngsters to empty its contents in her purse, which was in the house.

Adults stopped on their way to work; some with time to spare, sat down to eat on the bench and table. Taxi cabs frequently made stops for either the driver or occupants to buy breakfast. Benskinuers, the motorbike taxi drivers lined up their bikes every morning, making it their first stop to fortify their stomachs before riding off to an unknown future, unsure if they'll make it back home alive. Sometimes it was a meeting spot for business people to meet and chat over breakfast.

Mama Sango was known all over Abakwa and beyond, especially for her fluffy puff-puff. Sometimes customers drove ten miles from Aziri to Ntamulung just to buy puff-puff. Quite frequently, indigenes brought their foreign guests from as far as America just to sample her cooking. Occasionally, visitors from abroad who had grown up eating her staple would come back to reminisce about the good old days. Jesse was one such visitor. He had arrived in Abakwa the night before and, in spite of the jet lag, couldn't wait to eat Mama Sango's beans and puff-puff. Against his mother's protests, Jesse mounted a *benskin*, the motorbike taxi, to Ntamulung Junction.

Shrieks of joy could be heard around the block, as Mama Sango hugged him. She held on to him for a moment, then held him at arm's length, inspecting him from head to toe with a wide smile. She was clearly excited to see him.

"You have grown so much into a handsome young man," she commented. "How are you, when did you come, for how long?" The questions flowed successively, without pausing for an answer. She secretly wished Jesse would ask for Marie-Noel's hand in marriage. After all, they had gone to the same school. She was just a class behind him and both had played hide and seek together!

*   *   *

It was almost nine thirty. The customers had dwindled, and the last of them bought all the remaining food. Mama Sango cleared the utensils. The fire can was the most difficult to move. It was a tin can of about sixteen inches in diameter and a two-foot tall cutout from a tar container with an open top and a six-inch hole close to the bottom for ventilation. The fuel was sawdust, compacted around two large bottles—one upright in the center of the open top, and the other, horizontally in the center of the cutout hole. Once the can was completely filled with compacted sawdust—moistened for cohesion—the bottles are retracted, leaving a hole perfected by the shape of the bottles. To start the fuel-generating process, a lit piece of wood is inserted in the horizontal hole, igniting the sawdust in the process. The horizontal hole served as an air intake, and the vertical as exhaust for the flame and heat, thus completing the cooking process. She lifted the hot handle with a stick, stuck her hand into a thick heat-resistant glove, and carried the brimming container behind the house. A couple of men still sat on the bench, chatting and eating their breakfast, not offering to help.

*   *   *

Mama Sango did not realize how full her bladder was as she concentrated on frying the puff-puff. The pressure on the bladder made it difficult for her to walk. It was daylight, and the possibility that someone might see her easing herself in the open was a risk she was not willing to take. She wheeled herself between three banana trees, and positioned herself with one leg raised over a banana tree stump. Using her right hand, she raised her Kaba from behind, and with the left, she expertly slid her underwear to the side. Then she let herself go. Anyone seeing her from the front would have no idea of what she was doing. Beads of perspiration appeared on her forehead. The relief was palpable. The thirst returned with a vengeance. Her lips were parched, and the urge to drink was uncontrollable. She felt a little dizzy.

"I must go to the hospital," she muttered to herself.

*   *   *

She was lost in thought as she held open the door to the refrigerator, pondering what to cook before she left for the hospital. Suddenly, she remembered! Sango loved her Jollof rice.

Today is going to be a good day, she thought. "I will surprise him," she said to herself.

She expertly cut the tomatoes into the pot with heating oil. A sizzling sound could be heard each time a slice of tomatoes dropped in the pot. The aroma from the combination of tomatoes, onions, celery, and seasoned beef made the mouth water. She smiled to herself as Sango's excited face appeared in her mind's eye.

She let the stew simmer, while the rice bobbled on the other burner. She quickly let go of the cover and watched it bounce off the stove on to the floor, spin in a wobbly pattern, before coming to rest on one side. In her absentminded state, she had forgotten about the cracked pot handle that exposed part of the stainless steel, which came in contact with her flesh. She grimaced in agony, shaking her hand in semicircular motions. The pain seemed to increase with the twirling. She stopped to examine the damage. Two lines of about half an inch wide were visible across her middle and ring fingers. The pain was searing, burrowing deeper into her flesh. She instinctively put the burnt fingers in her mouth, and then she remembered the eggs! She smeared some slimy, raw egg white on the burns, instantly relieving the discomfort.

Mama Sango lowered the flame and spread the marinated sauce all over the rice. The water in the pot had been absorbed, with steam emanating from visible pores on the rice surface. The pores provided an avenue for the sauce to migrate to the bottom and back up again, spreading through the rice in the process. She let it simmer for a little longer then stuck a fork through the rice up to the bottom of the pot. Pulling it out revealed a clean fork, an indication that all the water had evaporated. Mama Sango stirred the rice, producing a uniform-colored blend of rice and stew. Cooking Jolloff rice was not an exact science. As with all Abakwa cuisine, there were no measurements for the ingredients, but miraculously, almost all the dishes tasted exquisite. Jolloff rice, however, stood in a category of its own. Sometimes, the outcomes are perfect; and sometimes, the result is a soggy mess!

Today's cooking was perfect. She scooped a spoonful, brought it up to her lips, took a deep breath, and cooled it with her breath. It was fluffy and delicious. She nodded to herself. She served Sango's dish and then Pa Sango's.

She then served two extra dishes, knowing full well that Sango would invite David and Stephen, his closest friends, to share the best Jolloff rice in the whole world that was prepared by *his* mother, the best cook in Abakwa.

6

THE LAST WISH

Mama Sango took a minute to admire her naked self in the full length mirror. She examined her face, moving closer to the mirror. A few wrinkles were evident under her eyelids. *That must be from lack of sleep*, she consoled herself. Her youthful breasts were still round and firm—something she thanked God for every time she was amongst her friends, all whom needed bra support. She wore them only to stem the unwanted attention from men staring at her prickly nipples.

She turned sideways, spinning on her toes and swinging her hips, hands on her waist. Her sideways pose showed her symmetrical body, as if God had taken the extra time and care during her creation. Her figure was like an elongated *S*. She looked at the dark bush that grew beneath her belly button. Pa Sango loved the look of it. He forbade her from cutting the hair, which he twirled around his fingers, sensually arousing her prior to lovemaking. She reminisced. The moist between her thighs brought her back to reality.

"Where are you?" she asked, softly. She lay down on the bed, unable to quell the flaming desire welling up inside her. She slowly dialed his number. This was strange. She hadn't had this longing for a long time. The rings were agonizingly long. Then his booming outgoing voice mail came up. She sighed.

His absence did not dampen her imagination. She imagined his arms around her; his breath sensual, longing, imploring. She clung tightly, spreading wide and moaning. Her gyrations were slow at first then progressively gained momentum, with hips swinging from left to right, raised off the bed, looking like a gymnast arching backward. The motions and moaning intensified. She sunk her nails and teeth into his soft flesh. There was a long scream, muffled by the tissue in her mouth, as feathers from the pillow flew all over the bed when she came to. Beads of perspiration appeared on her forehead as she lay there, spent. She would have spent the rest of the afternoon in bed, if she hadn't promised herself to go to the hospital.

*   *   *

She admired herself in the mirror, this time fully dressed. Satisfied, she picked up her purse, and walked out of the room. The family portrait caught her attention as she prepared to exit the house. She moved closer. Her gaze fixed on Sango, her pride and joy. She admired him in his dark grey suit, the one his aunt Marie-Noel had sent for his fifth birthday. How Marie-Noel knew to buy clothes that just fit baffled her. She stood there, lost in thought.

"You will go to America," she half told herself, running a finger down the length of his portrait. She smiled, turned around, and walked out.

7

THE LAST RIDE

The taxi driver slowed down, obeying the command of Mama Sango's outstretched arm with an extended forefinger. She continued in her stride, her back to the oncoming traffic and without a care in the world as to whether the car she was stopping was a taxi or not. She was dressed to kill. The taxi driver could not help but marvel at the exquisitely dressed woman hailing a taxi. Such women belonged to the high society in affluent communities in subdivisions like Up Station Senior Service Quarters, where the *who's who* of Abakwa lived.

From behind, she looked like one of the models found in a magazine spread. Her white blouse was perfectly tucked into her red skirt that extended just below her knees, exposing her long, caramel-toned legs. Her calves were firm, emphasized by the red high- heeled shoes she was wearing. Half of her straight brown hair lay on her back, and the other half tucked underneath her hat. The hat was elongated like a fire fighter's with a red band around the protruding part. The sun cast a little shadow on her face, highlighting her soft-colored sunglasses.

"Mama Sango, is that you?," asked Johnny, the taxi driver. He leaned down, his head almost touching the steering wheel. "*Cheih*, Mama Sango, Jesus of Nazareth," he exclaimed. "Mama Sango, if I didn't know Pa Sango, I would have pursued you till thy kingdom come."

"Where are you headed?" he asked.

"To the hospital. I have not been feeling well these days," she replied, as she took the front seat. The lady passenger in the back suddenly felt intimidated and a little envious, for all the attention she had prior to meeting Mama Sango suddenly vanished, making her feel inconsequential.

The two-lane streets of Abakwa were crowded. It was midafternoon, and civil servants were returning to their offices after the lunch break. The hustlers were hawking their wares, while taxi drivers honked indiscriminately as pedestrians dodged the dangerous omnipresent motor-bikes. Mama Sango smiled sadly, as she reminisced about the good old days when Abakwa's streets were clean and organized. Motorbikes were a rarity then; now, they control the streets. University graduates aspired to have prestigious jobs then; now they aspire to be motorbike drivers—educated, driven, and reckless.

The taxi pulled over close to the hospital entrance gate. Cars were not allowed through the gates except in emergency situations. Mama Sango climbed out, turning heads in the process. The peanut huckster appeared mesmerized. A gentleman in a dark blue suit was captivated, walking straight into a puddle while staring at her. Mama Sango was well aware of the attention her beautifully dressed shapely figure commanded. She silently thanked her sister, Marie-Noel, for the body-defining clothes.

8

THE HOSPITAL

Mama Sango was seventh in line to be consulted. She sat on the wooden bench, next to an older grandmother who appeared to be having stomach cramps. She was not medically inclined, but she deduced the diagnosis by observation. The grandmother's scarf was tied tightly around her stomach and knotted around her navel. As if the tight scarf was not enough to stem the discomfort, her hands were folded around her stomach with her body arching over them. Her head was downcast and rose occasionally every time someone was called into the consultation room.

Mama Sango sat with legs crossed, looking sophisticated. Although she knew almost all the patients and nurses, most did not recognize her immediately. The contrast between the puff-puff frying, beans-cooking Mama Sango and the one sitting in front of them was irreconcilable. Most had never seen her anywhere else, besides her business location, dressed in her kaba and apron. They appraised her with genuine respect.

A young girl was brought in, literally being carried by two young men and supported on the bench on both sides. She moaned constantly, breathing heavily.

"What's wrong with her?" asked Mama Sango, leaning slightly forward to get a line of sight in front of the other patients.

"She has malaria," replied one of the young men.

Mama Sango sprang to action instinctively. From experience, she knew there was no running water in the hospital. She dashed down five flight of stairs to the vending stand a hundred feet away, high heels notwithstanding. She bought a plastic one-liter Tangui bottle. The swiftness and efficiency of her actions stunned the observers. She pulled out a white handkerchief from her purse, poured cold water on it, and dabbed the face of the sick woman. She waved off the young man sitting on the bench on the left side of the woman, straddling the bench in the process. She carefully wheeled the young woman's body around, leaning it on her bosom.

She continued to wipe the woman's face and gradually edged down to her neck, chest, and arms. She lifted the woman's chin up. Her eyes were half-closed. She placed the woman's chin between her thumb and index fingers and gently squeezed her jaws. Her patched lips opened, showing four spiderlike strands of saliva—a telltale sign of dehydration. Mama Sango poured a little bit of water down her mouth. Her half-opened eyes rolled left, then right, and back up. She swallowed the water and then whimpered.

"Thank you," she whispered feebly.

Mama Sango placed the back of her hand on the woman's forehead. The burning temperature was subsiding.

"Call the nurse," she ordered, her voice two decibels above normal. Her tone was stern, urgent. "This lady needs immediate attention," she told the nurse standing in the doorway, leaning on the frame with her left wrist bent backward on her waist.

"Don't tell us how to do our job. We'll get to her when we are ready," the nurse replied and walked back inside.

Mama Sango could feel her heart missing a beat. She looked like a woman possessed. The only thing her blood-shot eyes saw was her mother lying there, lifeless. Years ago, reckless nurses had taken their time, not bothering to attend to her mother, while she lay convulsing from a malarial attack.

A male nurse wheeled a wheelchair toward the young woman just as Mama Sango was rising, fists clenched and veins visible on her forehead. The male nurse smiled and said hello to everyone, unaware of the tension his affection-ate compassion had just defused.

Mama Sango took a deep breath. A *whoosh* could be heard as she exhaled. Her heart thumped against her rib cage, and beads of perspiration appeared in her palms. She felt a little dizzy and thirsty. Without much thought, she gulped down the rest of the water in the bottle.

Oops! The urge to use the bathroom was sudden. *Oh God*, she thought. Where would she relieve herself? The con-ditions of the hospital toilets were abysmal. She remem-bered the last time she visited. The humid weather made the stench emanating from the toilets suffocating. On that occasion, she wore loose clothes and had no difficulty hid-ing behind the little building to urinate. This time around, there was no such luck. She was dressed to the tee, and the thought of performing that feat did not occur to her. Could she hold it? No telling how long she was going to be wait-ing in line for her turn to see the nurse.

"Could you please reserve my place for me?" she asked the woman next to her. "I will be back shortly."

"Sure," the woman replied.

Mama Sango took measured steps, conscious of the pressure that was beginning to build in her bladder. Lately, the demands on her bladder had been immediate. The intervals between the sensation and the urge to use the bathroom were minimal, and she was now becoming an expert at figuring out how to react to her urges. Her measured steps quickened, though deliberate. She crossed the street to Mama Angie's stall next to her house. Mama Angie was sitting behind the counter, doing what she did best: peeling oranges with a small penknife that produced intricate designs.

"Eh, eh, Mama Sango. They say a toad never runs in broad daylight without something chasing it. What brings you here at this time of day, ma sister?" This was not the time for discussions.

Mama Angie pointed out the way to her bathroom. With mounting pressure, Mama Sango fumbled with the button. Her legs were now crossed in an attempt to stop the leak from becoming a downpour. In all the anguish, she had completely forgotten that all she had to do was pull up her skirt and she'd be free.

Mama Sango was thankful for her friend's help, as the pressure on her bladder was released. She still felt a burning sensation even after the gush ebbed. "This cannot continue," she told herself. "What is wrong with me? I am not that old, why is my bladder getting weaker every day? Why this burning sensation? Do I have an infection? Is Pa Sango faithful? It was a week and a half ago that we made love. Why has he been coming back late lately?" Congosa, the voice inside her head, took over. She imagined him with another woman. The voice within was very convincing, conjuring up vivid images. "Pa Sango!"

The sound of her voice bouncing off the tiled walls startled her. How long has she been sitting there? She stood up calmly, rebuking the devil that was her self-talking head for attempting to pollute her mind against her loving husband.

Two patients behind her had been called in for consultation. Luckily for Mama Sango, a few of the patients who were there when she left identified her, so they let her back in on the line. She sat down, crossing her legs around the ankles. A few yards down the opposite hallway, a woman was writhing in pain. Then it dawned on her that the majority of the patients—the ones mostly in pain—were women. Why, she asked herself? Congosa, the voice within, began again, analyzing and reanalyzing with plausible and implausible outcomes.

9

THE TRAGEDY

"**M**ama Sango," called the nurse. *Finally*, she thought. She stood up elegantly and walked into the consultation room with an uncommon gait. Her back was straight, shoulders squared, and head cocked to the side. Her handbag hung on her left hand, right by the elbow of her forearm. Her left wrist was slightly turned downward, revealing her rose-colored Cover Girl fingernails. Her Avon fragrance wafted through the room, masking the pungent smell of spent gauze, made unsavory to the eye by the color of iodine.

Nurse Loveline immediately disliked her. The hostility was subtle but evident. "What brings you here today, madam?" she asked condescendingly.

Mama Sango smiled, ruefully, determined not to stoop to Nurse Loveline's level. "For the past two weeks, I've been having frequent headaches, drinking, and urinating a lot. Sometimes I feel dizzy, but it lasts for a short time and then goes away. I don't have the appetite to eat as I used to a few weeks ago."

"It seems like you are losing a lot of electrolytes through dehydration. Since you are not retaining the water you drink, we will hydrate you intravenously and then send you to the lab for a blood test. The doctor will see you after your results are in," responded Nurse Loveline.

Nurse Loveline looked fiftyish, plump, and voluptuously endowed. She reminded Mama Sango of one of the cartoon characters she saw in one of Sango's many cartoon books that her sister, Marie sent from the US, broad-chested at the top but tapering down to a tiny waistline. She walked as if her disproportionate upper body was too much for the lower, forcing the lower to be constantly in motion while the upper stayed immobile. *She must be very experienced*—or so Mama Sango thought—*to have come up with a diagnosis without tests or even a blood pressure or pulse check.*

Mama Sango lay on the stretcher bed and waited to be hydrated intravenously. Her hat and bag hung on the coat rack a few feet away. She felt uneasy, lying on the cold brown stretcher. She watched as Nurse Loveline went around, preparing the solution that was to be her medication.

"Something is not right about this woman," Congosa, the voice within, lamented. "First of all, she was rude when you requested help for a very sick patient and was rude to you when you came in. Should she be the one giving you medication? I don't like her."

"She is a nurse and is supposed to be professional about it. She is doing her job. Besides, she is the only one here." Mama Sango convinced herself.

Nurse Loveline injected some clear medicine drawn from a small vial into the IV hanging on the mobile cart. She gave the cart a little push and smiled down on Mama Sango. She pulled out a pair of light blue rubber gloves from the metal drawer to the left of the stretcher.

Mama Sango noticed the rust on the front of the drawer and wondered how the interior looked like.

Nurse Loveline put on the gloves, smiling all the time. She pulled closer to her patient, revealing a pronounced cleavage as she bent down slightly while pulling the stool closer. She lifted Mama Sango's right arm, carefully examining it as if there was something unbecoming or out of place. After what seemed like an eternity for Mama Sango, Nurse Loveline tied an elastic tourniquet around her arm just above the elbow. Nurse Loveline curled her stout middle finger and placed it against the flat surface of her thumb with enough pressure that when released, stung Mama Sango's flesh. Fortunately, Mama Sango's constant lifting of her utensils and sacks of food made it easy for Nurse Loveline to locate the correct vein.

Nurse Loveline cleaned the area with alcohol and dried it with sterile cotton. She unscrewed the cap of the needle, and with the dexterity of an experienced nurse, inserted the IV catheter through the skin at an angle of about 30 degrees into the vein. Blood spurted through the needle into the IV pouch hanging on the cart. With the right hand holding the needle in place, Nurse Loveline placed a Band-Aid over the needle with her left hand, securing it to Mama Sango's arm. She then adjusted the flow of the liquid, and the blood started disappearing back into Mama Sango's arm.

10

MARIE-NOEL

The phone rang incessantly. The rings sounded distant, a consequence of her stage two REM sleep. Marie-Noel was too tired to get up from her bedroom. She knew the call was from back home. She had set it up that way. The landline was reserved for home calls, so she could answer when she wanted. She was just back from a double shift, and her feet ached. Her body was out of sync with her mind. It refused to budge when her mind instructed it to get out of the car, get in the house, and get to bed.

The night's events flashed through her mind as she sat in the driveway in front of her beautiful home, contemplating. Stella, the DON (Director of Nursing) had not been very helpful, which made for a long night. *How condescending*, she thought about the way Stella talked to her...and then came the knock on her car window that disoriented her. Mr. O'Brian, her next-door neighbor was out on his morning walks and saw her slumped against the car door, sleeping the morning away. It was now 8:15 a.m., forty-five minutes after she got home.

Home to Marie-Noel—still single at thirty-two—was a 3,800 sq. ft. single-story building with an immaculately trimmed lawn, located in an upscale Potomac neighborhood in Maryland. The intricately designed awning, hovering over the main entrance, signaled to any visitor that the occupant had *arrived* and that the American dream was no longer elusive.

Marie-Noel worked hard, sometimes working two shifts at two consecutive jobs. There were periods where she would not see her beautiful home, let alone sleep in her plush bed for a whole week! She was literally working herself to death. It seemed like a perpetually recurring nightmare. The early morning calls for help from home seemed to occur more frequently since graduating from nursing school. Was it her fault? Did she encourage it by giving in to the demands too easily? Was she being conned of her hard-earned money? The self-talk became more conspiratorial. The bills did not stop either. The harder she worked and earned, the faster her income dissipated.

Though childless, Marie-Noel supported three children at home; Sango, her sister's only child; Precious, her second cousin; and Divine, her best friend, Geraldine's son. Precious and Divine were optional. Sango, on the other hand, was not. Sango was *her* son. *She* was the one who helped her sister give birth to him. *She* was the one who cut the umbilical cord! That was ten years ago, but she remembers it like it was yesterday.

11

THE BIRTH

Her sister cried out. It was a terrifying shriek. Marie-Noel was immobilized by the terror—a crippling kind of terror instigated by long forgotten memories. The sight of the liquid gushing out of her sister unto the floor reminded her of the incident and completely paralyzed her, until a direct order to get Mama Alice, the neighbor down the road jolted her out of her trance. She bolted like lightening, crossing the pothole-filled gravel road without checking for oncoming traffic, narrowly escaping what would have been a catastrophe. Thankfully, the cab driver's active and artful dodging of potholes—an unintended but welcomed outcome—saved her life.

Mama Alice sprinted with the agility of a teenager, pulling the wrapper cloth up to her knees with her left hand, freeing up her legs to pedal forward. She dashed into the room where Mama Sango sat on the floor, overcome with pain. With Marie-Noel's help, they got Mama Sango to the bed. With razor-like hands, Mama Alice ripped the clothes off Mama Sango, exposing her belly stretched thin by the enormous bulge, seemingly held together by a black line starting from her belly-button down to her private area.

Mama Alice, the quintessential midwife, was used to these sporadic home deliveries. She came prepared, as if she expected the call! She placed all the pillows in the house behind Mama Sango, gently pushing her backward, to an angle of about 30 degrees. Without washing her hands, Mama Alice doused rubbing alcohol in her cupped right hand and rubbed it on both hands vigorously. She put on rubber gloves retrieved from her blue-leather child-birthing kit. She spread other utensils on the bed beside Mama Sango, gently spreading her legs as the contractions recommenced.

"Take a deep breath and push," she instructed, as she inserted her middle and forefinger, one on top of the other, into Mama Sango. With circular motions, she made several revolutions around the mouth of the vagina with the fluid as lubricant. "Now this is it. I can see the head. Take a deep breath aaand push."

Veins were visibly popping on Mama Sango's forehead. She took a long deep breath and with clenched teeth, gave one final push. Marie watched from the side, crying for her sister's pain. When the baby's head popped out, Mama Alice expertly guided it, gently turning the baby to the side as it slid out.

"It's a boy," she said calmly.

Mama Alice suctioned out some fluid from his mouth, flipped him over, and gently tapped him on the back. Screams of protest came shortly after with the rising and falling of his tiny rib cage. Mama Alice gently placed the baby on his mother's bosom. With patched lips and face drenched in sweat, Mama Sango cry-laughed or laugh-cried. Tears of joy streamed down her face as faint laughter could be heard in the mix. Mama Alice continued to clean the baby.

"Here, auntie,"—Mama Alice motioned to Marie-Noel, handing her the scissors—"you cut the cord."

12

THE INCIDENT

Marie-Noel's affinity for her sister grew stronger after Sango's birth. Theirs was a special bond, cemented by events of the past—a past that was fraught with pain.

Years ago, Marie-Noel came home from school one afternoon to find her sister, Chastity lying unconscious on the floor in a pool of blood. How she got back to school to get her dad, who was the principal of Njinikom, Presbyterian Secondary School, remains a mystery. She clung to him tightly as they rode back home on his motorbike at breakneck speeds, bouncing in and out of potholes that littered the street. He took one look at his daughter on the floor and understood.

As luck would have it, his wife, Mama Marie rode with her friend to work that morning. Pa Forgoodness backed up the car to the house and gently placed his daughter on the pile of towels in the backseat of the car. "You stay here and wait for your brother," he instructed Marie-Noel.

Dr. Happy was relieved the day was almost over. He hung his white coat on the gold-plated hook on the back of the medicine cabinet in his office. He sat down and started examining the pile of paperwork on his desk. Then came the frantic calls and cascading footsteps. Three hours later, he emerged from the OR (Operating Room) with some good news for the principal, Pa Forgoodness and his wife.

"Thank you for acting fast. Things would have been different if she didn't get here when she did. Everything went well. My only concern is, she may never bear a child again," he said.

Pa Forgoodness, uncharacteristic for a man of his caliber, was overcome with emotion. "Thank you, Jesus. Thank you, Jesus. THANK YOUUU, JESSSUS," he screamed as he slid down the wall, squatting on the bare concrete floor, fists clenched upward, and tears streaming down his furrowed face.

*   *   *

Marie-Noel was ecstatic to see her sister a week later. Pa Forgoodness showed an uncommon compassion for his daughter after the *incident.* Was it because of the fear of losing *his* oldest child?

Chastity healed slowly. No one discussed the *incident* at home. They all understood. It was a secret—an open secret. Pa Forgoodness was shaken to the core. Colleagues noticed a change but couldn't bring up the courage to ask why. Mama Marie was numb with pain but made fresh vegetable soup every morning for her daughter before leaving for work. Her friend noticed her reticence. The secret stayed a secret, until Nurse Prudence at the clinic blabbed about it to a friend. Then the story dripped and dripped and dripped some more, until it became a gush, with everyone around the town having a fill of it. Chastity became a household name and a topic for daily musings. Furtive looks accompanied her everywhere she went. She could feel the eyes behind her back; she could hear the silent conversations. Her so-called friends steered clear of her and avoided her like a plague. All her friends...except one. Patience.

Patience paid her a visit. She did not ask. The meeting was awkward at first, but then they warmed up and carried on where they left off before the incident, as if nothing had happened. As they walked together on the path to part ways, Patience put her right arm on her friend's shoulder. They were of differing heights, so the walking became cumbersome. Patience slowed down, stopped, and then turned around to face her friend. She put both arms around her and said, "I am here for you. If you need me, let me know. I love you."

Chastity burst into tears, convulsing with the release of pent-up embarrassment. Her shoulders heaved repeatedly as she curled, squeezing her stomach as if to flush out whatever was ailing her. Patience held her up and embraced her tightly, rocking her from side to side. They both cried. Chastity was three months shy of graduating from secondary school. She was a straight A student with high ambitions. Beauty, wit, and charm kept the boys fawning and the girls envious. The girls saw an opportunity after the incident to pounce, tearing her down with reckless abandon. For the first time in her life, Chastity felt lonely. Her grades slipped, and doubt crept in.

The pressure was unbearable. The embarrassment and shame she felt for having soiled the name of her prestigious family was overwhelming. How could an innocent encounter turn into such a disaster? They'd both met at the public tap. He was behind her in line. She could not get the lid off the twenty-liter container when it was her turn to fill up.

He helped her. A week later, they met at school. He waved, she smiled and waved back. He timed his water-fetching trips to coincide with hers. They talked and exchanged notes at school. Her father was the principal and a strict disciplinarian. His was a shoe repairman. Theirs was an unlikely union.

The courtship blossomed. Her heart ached if a day went by without them seeing each other. They concocted all kinds of excuses and created opportunities to be close to each other, even just within eyesight. The relationship progressed, and soon, Chastity was sneaking out the window in the dead of night to be with Precious under the pear tree. They talked a lot about nothing. The first kiss was magical. She could literally see stars with her eyes closed. His eyes were the only thing she saw when she closed hers during the nightly family prayer. One thing led to another, until they could wait no longer.

They both came prepared; Chastity with nothing underneath the black nightgown, and Precious with some lubricant. The thick foliage under the coffee tree provided a good cover for their first sex act, and it soon became a nightly event except for the nights when Pa Forgoodness would stay up late and it would be too dangerous for her to sneak out.

Three months later, Chastity missed her period. She didn't think anything of it. A month later, she missed the second one. Alarm bells rang, and both teenagers became frantic. Her father would skin her alive! Precious disappeared for two days. On the night of his return, he gave her the mixture. She was to drink all of it before she went to bed. Because the fetus was still forming, the concoction would dissolve it and be passed out as a normal bowel movement event the next morning. Chastity did not feel well that morning and asked to be excused from school. She was alone when the full force of the mixture she had consumed hit her, and the last thing she remembered was crawling to get to the phone, to call for help.

That April Fool's Day was a fateful one—a day that changed the course of Chastity's life for good. She had planned it well. Not even Marie-Noel, her closest confidant, could be confided in. Chastity had not given much thought to where she was going. All that preoccupied her mind was getting away. In place of the thick text books, she packed just the basics in her book bag, so no one would notice. With 48,000 CFA she had saved from her allowance, Chastity boarded a taxi and drove into the unknown.

13

THE FOREBODING

Marie-Noel was still groggy as she wobbled from the bed to the bathroom, sheets wrapped around her for comfort. She vaguely remembered the phone rings as she sat on the commode; hands resting on her knees, supporting her throbbing head. She decided she needed more sleep. She didn't want to hear any bad news that would interrupt her sleep. The week had been rough, and she looked forward to resting the next three days.

Restless in bed, she wished he were there. Half-asleep, she stretched out her hand to where he would be, gently caressing the satin sheets he so loved sleeping on. "Bright," she whispered. *Was he at work, school, or at home*, she wondered. Then it crossed her mind, the thought she dreaded but couldn't resist. Was he seeing someone else? The last time they were together, he had complained about her work schedule and the strain in was putting on their relationship.

"Slow down," he had said. "You'll work yourself to death, Marie. Don't end up like Mercy. She died from exhaustion at the traffic light after working a triple shift! I don't see you anymore. All you do is work, work, work. You're going to die, and the work will still continue." She could see his smiling face, and that was the last thing she remembered.

The doorbell rang once, paused for a minute or so, and then rang again; this time, continuously, forcing her to get up. *Who the heck is this?* she thought! She recognized his SUV parked in the driveway. "What's chasing you?" she asked, not too excited about being rudely awakened.

He ignored her question, gave her a peck on the cheek, and walked right to the fridge.

There it was, the bottle of Heineken he had left the last time he visited. He grabbed it and fidgeted through the kitchen drawer for an opener. He took a long sip and sat down on the couch, opposite her.

She thought he was acting strange. "What's the matter with you?" she asked.

He smiled, apologetically.

"I was just thirsty," he said.

"When you are thirsty, you drink water not beer," she chided.

"Can a man just have a beer in peace?

His mind raced. How was he going to tell her? Forcing a smile, he said, "You look beautiful for someone just waking up."

"What do you want?" she asked, feigning annoyance. She folded her legs behind her, pulling the sheets over them as she lay on the couch. "Chinua Achebe said a toad does not jump around in broad daylight for nothing. So what brings you here in this hot weather?"

"I just assumed you'd be home after your marathon schedule, so I wanted to see you. I miss you, you know," he said, smiling.

She smiled, admiring his handsome face attached to his neatly trimmed head. He moved over to the couch, forcing her further into the couch and creating space for one buttock. They both felt the warmth of their touching bodies. He bent down to kiss her.

"Get your stinking breath away," she said, as she turned her face away from his beer breath.

"Let's go eat," he said, as he remembered his mother's wise counsel. "My son," she would say. "Never get out of the house without eating. If you can't eat, drink a glass of water. Because if you do leave the house without food and then hear that I died, you will not have the appetite to eat. I wouldn't want you to follow me from starvation," she reasoned.

He was going to fill her up before telling her. He took her to her favorite spot, Kitchen Near You in downtown Hyattsville.

"Oh, I left my phone in the car. Can I please use yours," he asked. He pretended to use it and turned it off as she went to the bathroom. It was better to be safe. He didn't want anyone springing the news on her.

"*Mami Nyanga!*" screamed Justice, the waitress, as she set the steaming plate of food in front of Marie. "How have you been?" asked Justice, pulling an empty chair so she could be level. They chatted for a little bit, and she appeared genuinely glad to see Marie. "How's Mama Sango? Do you hear from her?"

Bright's heart skipped a beat. He wished they would change the topic.

They exchanged numbers with Marie conveniently juxtaposing her last two numbers. "Let's catch up sometime," said Justice and left to attend to another customer.

"Catch up?" Marie muttered under her breath, rolling her eyes; her eyelids fluttering in the process. She emitted a long sigh while shifting from side to side on her seat, as she gestured her right hand at Justice's disappearing figure. "Me, catch up? Since when?"

"You need to let go of the past," he said. "See where she is."

14

THE ARRIVAL

It was fifteen years ago. Marie-Noel arrived at Dulles International Airport in the dead of winter. Her dream of going to America materialized through a complex set of schemes that culminated in her attending a conference on Empowering Women. Justice, her childhood friend was there with open arms, accompanied by Jason, her black American boyfriend. They hugged and danced, attracting the stares of the other passengers eager to pick up their luggage.

The ride home was full of chatter, as they reminisced about the past, laughed, and giggled like two prepubescent teens. The two-bedroom apartment was sparsely furnished, but whatever furniture present exhibited Justice's high taste. Marie-Noel's room was no different. The queen-sized bed, placed in the center of the room, was neatly made up with a matching nightstand to the right.

Strains in the relationship started materializing three months later when the flow of Marie-Noel's money dried up. With no source of income, Marie-Noel experienced an inexplicable uneasiness. She depended entirely on her friend for guidance and direction. Helpful information flowed freely within the first few weeks and then trickled as she overstayed her welcome. Fortunately, the never-ending social events, like the recurring Friday night cry-dies, provided an opportunity for Marie-Noel to meet new people. Her beautifully sculptured frame, supported by long healthy legs, did not disappoint. Her illuminating smile had a disarming effect on everyone she engaged with. The attention always turned from Justice to Marie-Noel unfailingly, glaringly, and repeatedly. Marie-Noel gleaned startup information from acquaintances that had been in her shoes. Nursing, the Holy Grail for most African immigrants, was the professional route of choice for advancement, through CNA, LPN, and RN—in that order.

Her first employment was under- the-table in a group home, owned by another immigrant from Abakwa. She was diligent and worked whenever she could. Her colleagues took advantage, calling off whenever they wanted. She worked doubles—sometimes triples—but making little financial progress. She was paid less than minimum wage. After all, she didn't have a work authorization, and Justice had demanded she pay half the rent. Catching the bus severely limited her ability to explore other opportunities. Had she known, she would have bought a car with the money she brought, instead of squandering it frivolously. Fortunately, it was springtime, and the biting-cold days became shorter.

Thanks to Bright, an acquaintance from one of those numerous social events, she was now enrolled in Prince George's County Community College, pursuing a GED certificate. She was heading in the right direction. The GED circumvented the need to prove she was a resident. Next in line was the CNA certification, which she passed with ease. Marie was poised for a career in nursing, as she prepared to enroll for the LPN course. Then all hell broke loose.

"Get out of my house now! Get out! Out," shouted Justice, completely naked and shaking violently, as she paced the distance between her room and Marie's.

Uncertain as to what was going on, Marie was dumbfounded. Mouth agape and words eluding her, her brain was unable to scramble them together. The look on Justice's face was scary.

"I can't believe you've been fucking my man behind my back. Why, why, why, Marie?" She sobbed, as she crumbled to the floor.

"Whaaat?" Marie-Noel finally muttered. "Justice, why are you saying that? I will never do such a thing."

In the background, Jason appeared, torso naked. "I'm sorry, honey. Nothing happened between us," he said, meekly.

"Don't touch me, you bastard. Don't you dare!" Justice screamed, recoiling. "I want you out." she turned to Marie. Her eyes turning to slits.

Marie fumbled as the tears welled up. Grabbing a travel bag, she tossed as many necessities as she could, stuffing a few crumpled dresses and shoes in the process. She was not willing to carry her suitcase, not knowing where she was headed. She picked up her lifesaving book bag. With a growling stomach, she took one final look at the pot of Jolloff rice she had just cooked not too long ago that was standing on the stove. With no appetite to eat, she stormed out of the apartment. She took the bus to the only other place she knew so well—her job.

"What's up, Marie?" asked Latoya, her colleague.

"I'm just coming back from out of town and didn't want to go all the way home before coming back here, so I'll just rest here," replied Marie.

It was 4:20 p.m. on a Thursday afternoon. Her shift didn't start till 11:00 p.m. Marie was thankful she had a place she could go to. Overwhelmed, she flopped on the bed and sobbed in the aid's room—the room that, unbeknownst to her, would become her refuge for the next eight months.

*   *   *

Having settled down in her new *home*, Mari-Noel went back to get her belongings from Justice's apartment.

"I am sorry, Marie" Justice said. "I overreacted."

Marie-Noel found Justice miserable, lonely, and wretched. She'd lost Marie and Jason, the two people she thought she knew well. But the damage was done. Marie was not prepared to come back after the humiliation. She was more determined to succeed. She promised herself that she would no longer live under someone else's control. Jason was the blessing in disguise she needed to fuel her drive. She forgave Justice, after learning the truth. Jason had committed the cardinal sin of calling Marie's name while passionately making love to Justice!

15

THE BOMB

DJ Skipper's music blared from the speakers on Abakwa's Commercial Avenue. It was about 4:25 p.m. during *Tory Time*, one of the most popular radio shows in Abakwa. Pedestrians marched to the beat, hucksters twirled in their makeshift sheds, and daily *buyam sellam* traders swayed on their stools behind their wares on the ground, occupying a full quarter of the street!

Abakwa was like a ghost town during *Tori Time*. The police chief wished every hour of the day and night was *Tori Time*. It was the only period when statistics proved crime went down. Lovers took a break from lovemaking, careful not to offend their partners for being distracted. Ba Tita, buying a gift for his wife, was 10,000 francs richer, a consequence of an absentminded Igbo trader's counting mistake. The streets were clear of the locustlike swamps of motorbike taxis. Everyone was engrossed in *Tori Time*. And then the music faded out, right at the moment when the singer was getting into the refrain.

"It's too late to apologi—"visibly irritating some listeners.

"Contry Pepo," indulged Akumbom Elvis McCarthy, Afrique Nouvelle's golden goose. His voice was somber, a contrast to his usually uncompromising bombastic routine. "Head tok for tori jus di enter for we tok tok house. Ma heart don tonam tonam, ma foot don shakeh-shakeh lekeh woman wrapper. Kontry Pepo, Mama Sango don sleep straight. The one and only Mama Sango, the original puff-puff and beans organizer for Ntamulung Junction don go for yonda. Ma belle di ton, ma hand di shake, water don cover ma eye. I no fit go before. If wuna see ma back, ma belle yi de for front. We go tory again ara time." (Fellow countrymen and women, it is with deep sadness that I announce the death of Mama Sango of Ntamulung Junction. News just reaching us indicates she died this afternoon. I am shaken to the core, and can't continue with this broadcast. We will next time around.)

*   *   *

Johnny screamed, unwittingly pushing down on the accelerator in the process and swerving into and out of the gutter, as he tried to avoid smashing into the car in front of him. As he finally regained control, he parked in the middle of the playground where the taxi came to rest, and sobbed like a child. His visibly shaken passengers consoled him; one of them joining in the weeping, overwhelmed by the driver's grief.

"I took her to the hospital two hours ago. How can this be? She was strong, full of life, and dressed beautifully. What happened? They killed her. They killed that woman!" he lamented.

The scene at Commercial Avenue was more chaotic. Horns blared as screeching cars avoided distraught pedestrians wailing at the top of their lungs, oblivious to the dangers they were putting themselves into as they agonized in the street. The news seemed to hit everyone at once, even Pa Sango! There was no escaping for him. In a health system with no set protocols for informing families in such tragic cases, Pa Sango heard from the radio—just like everyone else. Abakwa suddenly went from an eerily mindless and somber town to a hysterically agitated, grief-stricken metropolis. The atmosphere was reminiscent of the days of political strife. Only this time around, the antagonist was the incomprehensible and elusive death!

* * *

Ntamulung Roundabout was a sea of heads within minutes. Incredulous crowds jammed the street, meandering around Mama Sango's house in unsuccessful attempts at catching a glimpse of the dazed and lethargic Pa Sango. Every now and then, ear-piercing shrieks would perturb the atmosphere.

Aunt Mangwi, who had not been so kind to Mama Sango in life, was now visibly distraught. She cried uncontrollably, rocking Sango in her bosom from left to right. Mama Clara took charge. She asked for and got a handful of women to commit to cooking for the evening, directing mourners where to sit. There was no room for emotions.

Pa Forgoodness sat calmly in his rocking chair, tangentially placed beside the fireplace in his living room. His demeanor was the epitome of serenity, a stark contrast to Mama Marie's uncontrollable outburst of grief. Years ago, news of this caliber would have taken days to reach Njinikom. Nowadays, there was no trickled-down news. Everything was instantaneous. Everyone within reach of Afrique Nouvelle's airwaves heard at the same time, instantly and without warning! Pa Forgoodness' composure belied the volcano within, immobilizing him in the process. His feet were numb, his vocal cords constricted. He sat there, motionless, unable to console or constrain his wailing wife. That task was ably handled by Pa Tiku, their longtime neighbor.

Mama Marie sobbed in his arms, deflated by the anguish. Her heart-wrenching gasps and pleas to God were too much—even for Pa Tiku who gently laid his charge on the floor, as he sought to conceal his tears. Ma Tilda, Pa Tiku's wife arrived with a bowl of steaming peanuts mixed with dry corn. She placed the bowl on the center table and sat down beside her grief-laden friend on the floor. And the wailing recommenced in earnest.

Mama Marie's hands went from her sides, to her head, and up into the air. She buttocksed on the floor, bouncing all over like a slightly deflated Michelin balloon. It was an amazing sight to see her go from one side of the living room to the other on her buttocks with no propellants.

16

THE NEWS

The fish was sizzling. Marie-Noel didn't know if it was hot because of the pepper, or because it was hot hot. She nibbled on the fried plantain and scooped a forkful of green vegetable. Steam emanated from the small porcelain bowl of rice nearby. The meal was healthy and well-rounded—fried plantain, roasted fish, green spinach, rice, and stew. Bright had fufu, okra soup with a lot of goat meat, and a bowl of green spinach. He ate with gusto, masking the turmoil that raged within him.

"I dreamt about Mama Sango today," Marie began. "She was in a bus and stuck her head outside, smiling, waving, and telling me something I couldn't understand."

Bright's heart sank. Should he break it now? He decided against it. He listened intently, made light of it, and changed the subject. They chatted, laughed often, and were visibly happy in each other's company.

*   *   *

Back in the comfort of her luxurious home, Marie scooped out some ice cream from the container and expertly rolled it on the cone. When she was done, it looked like one of those in a magazine spread.

Bright watched as she sat on the couch, sensuously caressing the ball-shaped ice cream with her tongue and making slurping sounds in the process. As the disappearing ice cream reached the crunchy cone, he reached out and took Marie's right hand. "I've got something to tell you," he said.

Marie's mind flashed, seeing him kneeling down and asking for her hand in marriage.

"Something terrible happened this morning. Mama Sango is d-dead," he stammered.

An electric shock zipped through Marie, leaving her frozen in place with lips open, poised for a bite of the dropped ice cream cone. "Nooo," she screamed at the top of her lungs.

Bright held her tight. The agonizing screams filled the house as she writhed in spasms.

"Why, Mama Sango, why, why. Please God, why, why did you take my sister? Gawd, answer me. Why, why, why?" she moaned.

The crying went on unabated for an hour. Bright held her close, patiently, silently. As she laid her head on his shoulder, Marie-Noel felt deflated and looked lifeless, like a lump on the couch. The only sign of life was the slow rise and fall of her abdomen, made visible with the help of the dinner she had just had.

Marie-Noel was a zombie for the next two days. The career and the reputation she had worked so diligently to build suddenly became irrelevant. Bright was right. The world turned without her spinning the wheel. Work did not stop. Her boss offered condolences but did not close the business. Marie, the diligent, hardworking, dependable, and most valued employee's absence was inconsequential to the dynamics of the business life cycle. Marie recalled the last conversation she had with her sister. It was about two months ago. She had been just too busy with work to call back!

17

THE MORGUE

Three hours after the death announcement, a five-person delegation was en route to the Hospital to see the demise of Mama Sango for themselves.

Pa Sango sat in the front of the taxi. Piled in the back were Mama Clara; Aunt Gwen, Pa Sango's older sister; Uncle David, Mama Sango's uncle; and Pa Tabah, an Abakwa subchief. The mood in the car was somber. Except for the occasional comment about the Jazz music by the DJ on the radio, everyone was respectfully quiet. The mortician directed the delegation through the cold, dark, dingy morgue. They passed rows of three-tiered concrete slabs stacked with stiffened bodies. For the first time in over three hours, Pa Sango let out an agonizing scream and slumped to the floor, as he caught sight of his wife's lifeless body.

"My baby, my baby! Oh, my baby! Why, why now? I'm here to get you. Get up, get up!" he pleaded. He tucked his left hand under her neck, lifting her off the slab; and with the right, grabbed her in a full embrace and kissed her on the cheek. He held her tight, sobbing. Everyone watched, tears streaming down their faces. After what seemed like an eternity, he let her down, straightening the fluffy apronlike design on the white shirt she'd worn that afternoon. He brushed aside the strands of hair that crossed her face then cupped her cheeks in both hands. He placed her hands on top of each other across her stomach, then undid them and held her hands, stretching her fingers and intertwining his fingers in hers. He squeezed, but there was no reciprocity. He raised them and sobbed again.

"My baby, my baby, get up. Get up. God please, make her get up. Ahheee, eehh, it's cold in here, baby. Let's go home. Get up, get up."

18

THE FAMILY MEETING

It was 4:30 p.m., a whole hour after the scheduled family meeting time in Njinikom. The Abakwa delegation had been late, delayed partly by the increased police checkpoints. Saturdays were pay days for the security forces, a day when bands of threes and fours set up checkpoints right next to liquor stores. It was an open and well-known secret. Taxi drivers or drivers of any commercial vehicle were to fork over 500 francs, no questions asked. Noncompliant drivers were unnecessarily delayed—and that was the case for the Abakwa delegation. Ta Tabufor, the family successor, chaired the meeting.

"Ladies and gentlemen," he opened, "before we proceed, I'd like to call on Ma Frida to lead us in prayer. We have gathered here to deliberate on the tragedy that has befallen this family. In the days of our forefathers, children buried their parents; now, day in day out, we hear of parents tasked with the enormous burden of burying their children. We don't feel the pain when it happens to others; but when it knocks and enters and is lying down in our own house, the pain becomes real. While this loss belongs to all of us, I want to extend my deepest sympathies to Pa Forgoodness,

Mama Marie, and Pa Sango. Words cannot begin to express how I feel, and how I feel cannot begin to measure with what you are experiencing. With that said, I will like to say the focus of this gathering should be to give our dearly departed daughter a befitting burial. But before we start deliberating on the modalities, I will like to yield the floor to Pa Forgoodness."

"Thank you, Tabufor. Thank all of you for coming here and for sharing in our grief. On behalf of my wife and son-in-law here, I say thank you. We are really grateful that you have taken the time to come and help us bury our daughter. Words can't express how we feel, but all I can say is that God's time is the best. Only God knows why she left us the way she did. We can only trust and believe that even though we loved her dearly, God loved her even more. She is now in a better place, and all we can do is to pray that she rests in peace."

"Pa Sango, would you like to say something?" Ta Tabufor asked.

"Yes," he said. "My chest is hurting. I feel like my heart has been ripped out of me. These past few days, my mind has been wondering, asking questions I cannot find answers to. I encouraged her to go to the hospital. Now I wonder if that was the right thing to do. I wonder if she would be here if I had gone with her. I try to remember what I told her that morning. How could someone walk in the hospital and drop dead?"

"Those types of questions will never cease, because you will never find the answer. She is the only one who can give you that answer but cannot, because she is not here. My son, these things are incomprehensible to us mortals. But God knows best and will show us a way out of this. I know it's easy for me to say, but I won't be with you at night to feel the empty bed. I won't be with you when the boy asks for his mother. I won't be with you when everything is said and done and everybody goes back to their respective homes. But all I can tell you is that the Almighty God we serve will see you through this very difficult time. I can only share words of comfort and pray that you please allow us to comfort you," said Mr. Marty, cousin to Mama Sango.

"We need to set a date for the burial and then…" Ta Tabufor trailed off.

"Burial date? Why the rush to set up a burial date?" asked Mama Marie. "I have not heard a single person mention finding out what killed my daughter, and all you are worried about is burial? What killed her, can you answer me?" Mama Marie was visibly agitated as she stood up, tying her wrapper cloth tightly around her waist. "That was my baby, all right? Where did she go? They say to the hospital. You go to the hospital to get cured, not to die. What happened to my baby?"

"Mafor," entreated Tangieh Ntum, the maternal uncle. "Please have a seat, and let me say something. Last week or so ago, the bird flu came and wiped out my chickens. There was this one hen that was very strong. I thought she would beat it, but then she caught the flu. She tried to fight it but gradually gave up. Finally, she just laid down and died. Why do I bring this story, you may ask? I brought it up because I know that she got sick, I know and saw her struggle against the disease, and I saw her die. That was the natural progression. Our daughter's death is worse than that of that chicken! She took her own two legs, walked into that hospital, and died worse than a dog. Am I angry? You bet I am. I am very angry, and we should all be angry.

And that anger ought to be channeled into finding out what happened and if possible, hold all those responsible for her demise accountable. I know all of you will tell me about your Jesus Christ and Christianity, but before Jesus Christ and Christianity came, we had our ancestors and our customs and traditions. And those customs demanded that when something of this magnitude happens, we find out why. Then we go to our ancestors, seek their counsel, and appease them so that such a thing never happens again. So I am in total support of Mafor in finding out what happened to our daughter traditionally."

"Tangieh Ntum," said Pa Forgoodness, springing to his feet even before Tangieh Ntum finished his last word. "I respect your views, but I'm going to respectfully disagree with your approach. May I remind you that Chastity or Mama Sango, is my daughter! We raised her up in the church. She believed in Jesus Christ as her savior, and I know she would not want to go the route you want. Yes, there is tradition, but the Bible says give unto to God what is His and unto Caesar what belongs to Caesar. It is God's wish that she went when and how she did, and I don't intend to question God. So as the father, I will not have any traditional meddling in my family business. Marie-Noel has instructed us to have an autopsy done, and that is the only way we are going to find out what happened."

"Ntseh," Tangieh Ntum called out indignantly.

This was the first time, in what seemed like an eternity, that anyone had actually called Pa Forgoodness by his real name. Mama Marie was taken aback, now torn between standing up for her husband against what she perceived as a personal affront by Tangieh Ntum or supporting her uncle in the search for her daughter's *killer*.

"Maybe this Christianity thing and too much *book* made you forget where you came from and who you are talking to. Let me remind you that, traditionally, you have no voice and no authority on issues pertaining to our daughter here. You can go on with your Jesus Christ agenda. We will be going to Bamessing tomorrow to the traditional doctor and find out what actually happened to Mama Sango. And until we find out, there will be no burial taking place."

19

THE BLAME GAME

Back at Ntamulung Junction, the square had undergone a transformation. Volunteers moistened the dusty graveled square and swept the area clean. Amateur electricians rigged the entire junction with cabling, and fluorescent bulbs were perched on eucalyptus poles harvested from the environs without prior consent from the owners. Every night since the night of the death of Mama Sango, the square was closed to traffic—a spontaneous decision spearheaded by the *benskineurs*.

The atmosphere was reminiscent of a carnival with Loh Benson, the anointed cry-die animator, animating. Throngs of people—young and old, male and female—formed and danced in a huge circle, with five or six pairs of couples intermittently taking center stage to show off their dexterity and dancing prowess. Sometimes two or three people would take turns holding up Mama Sango's picture frames, circling around the dancing perimeter. The spot where Mama Sango sat and sold her famous puff-puff and beans had been turned into a shrine. The lone bench was placed directly behind the tin stove. A large framed portrait of her in action—courtesy of a client—leaned between the pot and the bench, as if to give an illusion of her actually sitting there, adorned with flowers. Some mourners swore they saw her sitting there in person. Some claimed they met her walking along the Ntamulung Junction street. The rumor mill was in full gear. Reported sightings were rampant, and then the rumor that her husband was the reason for her death took hold. A hush fell whenever and wherever her husband came within earshot. Some turned away surreptitiously to avoid eye contact.

"How could he sell his wife for money?" they whispered.

There was a rumor that he was trying to revive his business and unwittingly sought business loans from members of a secret society that traded money for souls. Once initiated by participating in their feasting, there was no turning back. The story goes that Pa Sango accompanied one of his friends to the secret meeting. The dinner was delicious. The red wine tasted so good, he asked for more and wanted to know where he could buy some for his wife.

"You can't find this in town." He was told. "If you want more, you'll have to become a member. Come back next week."

And so Pa Sango, goes the rumor, went back a second, third, and fourth time. On the fifth time, he was awarded the first installment of the loan he sought, two hundred thousand francs. On the seventh week, he was informed that he would be hosting the next time around.

"Can I bring something different? My wife makes really good beans and puff-puff."

There was a collective hearty laugh from the members. "The staple here is plantains and meat, just like what you have been eating all these weeks. You don't have to worry about cooking it. We have special cooks here."

Towards the end of the meeting, the story goes, Pa Sango was steered into a private room situated behind the meeting hall and separated by black linen. Suddenly, he found himself in a room full of people; some, he ascertained, had died a long time ago. They were all on a farm; some milking cows, others rearing goats, some splitting wood, while others cooked. He felt trapped in a trance he couldn't get away from. And then, out of nowhere, emerged his wife and son, smiling and waving at him. They were out in the open, separated from the busy workers by a fence, and waited patiently by the gates.

"You choose who goes in," instructed a deep voice.

It dawned on Pa Sango what he had gotten himself into. Unable to extricate himself from the trap, Pa Sango, as the rumor went, chose to sacrifice his wife.

20

THE VERDICT

The drive to Bamessing, which is thirty-five miles from Abakwa, was uneventful. Though the appointment was set for twelve noon, a decision was made to leave at 4:00 a.m. that Sunday morning. At that time of the day, the extorting police would still be in bed. The dust will be minimal, because all other commercial transporters will be off the roads. In short, they would have a smooth, straight ride without harassment. It worked.

They arrived at Bamessing in the wee hours of the morning and started the hour-long trek up the hilly, narrow winding path to Ma'Allam Nkwenti's home. From a distance, the corrugated zinc roof looked like a lone star in the midst of a thick, lush green forest. Up close, the tea plantation surrounding his house was beautifully serene, with the greenery providing a deep sense of tranquility. A half-moon welcoming sign adorned the handcrafted raffia palm entrance to a beautifully manicured lawn centered in front of the main building. On both sides of the main building were two smaller buildings, one for each wife and her kids. Judging from the majestic appearance of the compound, it must have been quite an undertaking for all the construction materials to be trucked up the hill.

Ma'Allam Nkwenti was a tall, handsome man with an easy gait. His black eye brows, coupled with the mustache surrounding his lips that meshed with his thick salt-speckled, neatly trimmed black beard, provided a nice contrast to his fair skin tone and the white robe he was wearing. He must have been in his sixties.

"Welcome," he said, extending his long arms and embracing each of his five guests. "Have a seat and feel at home," he added before disappearing into an adjacent room.

Soon after, his young beautiful daughter emerged with a tray of five small tea cups, handing one to each visitor. Her father followed with a kettle, pouring hot tea into the cups. Sugar was passed around and soon, everyone was enjoying the sweet aroma of Ma'Allam Nkwenti's fresh, handpicked tea leaves. Ma'Allam Nkwenti listened intently to the reason for the visit, nodding knowingly. He pensively stepped out of the room without a word, leaving his visitors wondering what was next. When he returned, three of his guests were asleep. Waking them up, he motioned for them to follow him. For about ten minutes, they filed after him through dense foliage and into a clearing with a small grass thatched hut. The handmade bamboo door was slightly to the right side of the opening. The opening was about four feet tall, so that everyone stooped down to enter the hut. It was dark inside. The only light was from a small window with a crosslike bamboo in the opening, tucked high on the ceiling. On the floor was a leopard skin spread to accommodate the Ma'Allam's hand-carved stool next to a black clay pot supported on three stones. On the skin were five cowries, darkened with age. Opposite the stool was a bench for the visitors.

Ma'Allam Nkwenti asked for and got a picture of the late Mama Sango. He placed it on the floor, next to the cowries. He picked up the cowries with his right hand, while the left was dangling down, supported by his left knee. He shook the cowries in small, circular motions and muttered to himself. He would bring them up to his lips in his cupped hand and gently blow into them. He threw them on the floor, and with his index finger, drew a series of perpendicular lines and pensively studied each one. He picked up an errant cowrie and muttered something to it before picking up the rest. He wiggled them once more, and threw them on the floor again. They followed the same pattern as before. He smiled to himself, saying nothing to the visitors. He threw them down a third time, and sure enough, they followed the same pattern.

He looked up, scanning the visitor's faces. "You are the husband?" he asked, gesturing toward Pa Sango.

"Yes." Pa Sango nodded.

"Why are you blaming him?" he said accusingly, looking at the others. "This man's hands are clean. I don't see anything that I can tell you." The drive back to Abakwa was long and eerily quiet.

*   *   *

Burial was set on a Saturday, two days after Marie-Noel's intended arrival. Preparations were in full force. Duties were assigned, and no stone was left unturned to ensure that Mama Sango was given a befitting burial. Ads were carried out on the radio and newspapers. A website was created in her honor and opened up for comments. Tributes came in from all over the world from individuals she had fed.

21

THE WAKE

B right cross-checked all the required visa documents and placed them in the FedEx envelope. Although they were within twenty miles of the embassy, they did not want to risk anything. They wanted tracked delivery documentation to and from the embassy. The official visa processing duration was seven business days, but there had been instances when two weeks was not enough, causing untold hardships. With the Washington DC area teaming with one of the largest populations of Cameroonians in the U.S., wakes were now a norm on Friday nights. Mama Sango's was just the latest. Justice was omnipresent. She stepped up, helping her "friend" in need. She became the chief organizer, ensuring that the menu at the wake was varied and plentiful.

Hard as she tried, Marie-Noel could not function. She walked around dazed and in a state of denial. Were it not for Bright and Justice, there would be no telling how she would have coped.

The Vikings Center in Burtonsville, Maryland was jam-packed with mourners, sympathizers, celebrants, and friends of both Marie-Noel and Mama Sango. A sizable number of the wake's attendees were former clients of Mama Sango's. Stories abounded of the delicious puff-puff and beans at Ntamulung Junction. Heartwarming tributes poured out, some about how they were fed despite not having the money to pay. Comical tributes made the evening lively, despite ending at 5:00 a.m. The population contributed handsomely, and at the end of the night, $13,865 had been raised!

Marie-Noel was aghast. She was overwhelmed with joy at the thought that her sister was loved by the people she touched. The fact that so many showed up to pay their respects was testimony to that. And she vowed to attend every wake she could and to contribute to all, regardless of the amount.

22

THE DEPARTURE

Marie-Noel boarded a Delta flight bound for Amsterdam from Dulles International Airport at 6:00 p.m. on a Wednesday evening. With a full schedule carefully planned out, she was determined to lay the groundwork to bring her sister's killer to justice. A call to Barristers Gilbert Bongam, Ann Tayuka, and Emma Akem yielded a road map and a sense of direction pertaining to the expectations. A month's vacation was too short a time frame for the Cameroon Justice system to yield any rewarding result, especially with the new frontier of a malpractice lawsuit, she gathered.

As the plane touched down on the Douala International Airport's runway, Marie became nostalgic. Tears welled up as she remembered the day she had taxied on the same runway years earlier on her maiden flight out of the country, while her sister waved frantically from the viewing towers. Instead of welcoming hugs, a cold casket with her remains awaited her. She imagined who would be amongst the delegation dispatched to welcome her back.

23

MARIE-NOEL'S ARRIVAL

A hot blast of putrid, humid air smacked her in the face, as she disembarked from the plane. As she gasped for air, she held on to the guardrail to regain her composure. She frantically sought fresh air, hoping against hope to find any crevice that would let in air from the outside. The walkway from the plane to the Custom's area was an airless tunnel. She could see the giant decrepit air ducts and wondered how long they'd been broken.

All of the other passengers were sweating. The Caucasian guy who sat two seats behind her was now four paces in front of her. His shirt was slung over his shoulder, exposing a T-shirt that almost blended with his pink skin. His face had turned red, partly because of the continuous wiping of drenching sweat.

Marie could feel the sweat in between her thighs. It was uncomfortable. As she approached the baggage area, she could smell the odors from unkempt armpits from afar and possibly other hidden areas. The baggage carousel, like the air ducts was also out of order. Luggage was trucked in on a flatbed cart. Miraculously, all her five bags made it on the same flight. It was not uncommon for a person's luggage to arrive on different flights on different days. Officially sanctioned, self-employed airport porters in green jackets and a name tag around their necks made themselves available, salivating at the prospect of earning much of their daily keep from this newly arrived American. While two of them haggled and heckled the tired and bemused Marie-Noel, a third saw a chance and took the initiative to load the luggage on his cart.

"Don't let him take your stuff," one of the hagglers implored.

"He's new here and doesn't know what he is doing. I can help you get through Customs easily. He's going to charge you a lot of money—"

"Sorry," Marie interrupted. "He's helping me already."

The young porter wheeled the flatbed kollli out of the chaotic luggage claim area. Midway to the Health Inspection area, he pulled the cart to the side, stopped, and turned around to face Marie for the first time.

Marie noticed the high cheekbones and strong facial features. His neatly twisted, dark, starter dreadlocks contrasted with his creamy complexion, but complimented by his neat beard and sideburns. He smiled, and his dimples were unmistakable. For a fleeting second, Marie's heart skipped a beat. He looked different from the other porters. Marie noticed the name on the tag he was wearing. His was a familiar Abakwa name. He was a recent graduate from the University of Buea trying to earn a living.

"I can help you get through Customs easily. With this amount of luggage, it may cost you 50,000 Frs if you go through the official route, but I can get it through for about 20,000 Frs."

His gaze shifted as Marie looked at him straight in the eyes, trying to determine if he could be trusted. She was aware of the corruption at the airport and had made a decision not to be part of it. "What if I don't pay?"

"Sister, trust me. You are from America. They know who is coming from America, and with all those boxes, you will be here all night. Sis, you can try if you want but just be ready for anything."

She had been traveling for almost twenty-four hours. She still had at least eight more hours to get to Abakwa. Did she have the luxury of time to combat these crooks? Wouldn't she be aiding and abetting this crippling criminal practice? But what would her stance accomplish in the large scheme of things? She would have won a small battle, but at what cost? The battle raged on within.

"Just wait here," he said, and disappeared around the corner with her Yellow Fever card and passport with 20,000 Frs in 5,000 Frs denominations tucked in the center. Marie debated if she had done the right thing by completely trusting a stranger with her travel documents. She could hear the silent recriminations in her head but decided to ignore them. Her attention turned to the ruckus that another traveler was causing not too far away.

"I am not paying a damn thing! You can keep me here all night if you want, but I can assure you, no one else is getting screened until you are done with me. What the hell is wrong with you people? I go out there and get treated badly. I come back home to my own country, and you are treating me like a criminal? Because you want a bribe from me? Hell no! You motherfuckers get paid for your job. Why didn't you check the other two passengers before me? Is it because they bribed you? They could be carrying weapons for all I care! Oh, but they walked right on with their luggage! Hell no! This nonsense is going to stop." She got out her smart phone and started videotaping as two officers approached her from the opposite end.

James, the porter, flashed two thumbs up as he approached Marie, smiling. Marie smiled back, her heart fluttering. He made a detour with the luggage, Marie in tow. He flashed a sign to the officers, and they all understood. The wheels had been properly oiled, now it was smooth sailing to the exit.

"My dear country," she muttered to herself.

A five-person delegation had been waiting outside the security area, peering and frantically waving through the glass barrier. Jude, her younger brother, and two cousins had been dispatched by the family to welcome her. As big as she thought she was, she felt like a kid again as Jude lifted her off her feet. They hugged each other tightly and rocked themselves from side to side, seemingly oblivious of the others.

"JJ, you've grown so big! You are now a man."

The scene outside the airport was chaotic. Peddlers were everywhere, hawking their wares and services. James was adept at clearing them out of his path, purposefully forging ahead with his load and forcing people to scamper off to the sides. James was on top of his game. He waived Eric Pofung, the driver, aside, and expertly packed the oversized boxes into the Pajero that was their carrier with more room to spare. "How much do I owe you?" Marie asked.

"Anything you have is fine with me, Sis."

She handed him 10,000 Frs.

"Do you have a card?"

"Yes," he said, handing her one.

"I will call you on my way back," she said, instinctively hugging him.

24

THE FUNERAL

The funeral procession was two miles long. It was presidential in scope. People lined the streets. Taxis drove at a snail's pace, led by the entire Abakwa motorbike taxis. It was surreal to see hundreds of *bendskineurs* riding in an orderly fashion and devoid of monetary ambitions, for the sole purpose of leading Mama Sango to her final resting place.

Ntamulung Presbyterian Church was filled to capacity. The population spilled out to the courtyard and the soccer field beyond. High turnout was anticipated and taken into account. Hundreds of seats were neatly arranged under huge tents. Loud speakers were strategically placed around the church's premises. The entire town appeared deserted—and for good measure. Mama Sango fed thousands of people over two decades with her specialty. The little school children she fed were now grown men and women all over the world. The senior divisional officer for Mezam was one such personality. The turnout at her funeral was evidence of the reach of her seemingly insignificant vocation.

The sermon was broadcasted live on private local radio and TV stations. This was the first of its kind in the entire province. It was unprecedented. The event provided a perfect avenue for educating the masses about diabetes and its effects, and Marie-Noel seized on the opportunity as she eulogized her sister.

*   *   *

"Hello, everyone! The first thing that comes to mind is *woah*! Looking at the sea of heads here, I didn't know whether to laugh or cry, whether to be happy or sad. But then I made up my mind a few minutes ago to be happy. I am just thrilled to know that my sister, Chastity—or Mama Sango as she is popularly known—was loved by all of you. I am sure she is very happy wherever she is, looking down on all of you here today for her sake. On behalf of my parents, my beloved nephew, Sango, his Dad, and my entire family, I just want to say thank you from the bottom of my heart. As my dad would tell you himself, it's never easy for a parent to bury a child. But I can tell you that he is so overwhelmed with the outpouring of love from all of you. Your support has made dealing with the loss easier, and for that, he is eternally grateful.

"I don't need to tell you, because you already know who she was; gentle, kind, beautiful with those curves, full of life, and above all, the best cook! All of you wouldn't be here were it not for her jazz—the best puff-puff and beans. She loved cooking and loved it more when all of you would finish your food and, in some cases, cleaned the bowls with your fingers. If it weren't for the good manners your mothers taught you, some of you would have cleaned the bowls with your tongues. She derived a great deal of pleasure from seeing you do that. She did so even to the last day of her life. She got up that morning and did what she always did—cooked her beans, fried her puff-puff, and fed the people. The only thing she did out of the ordinary that day was visit the hospital. We have all heard varying versions of how she died and what killed her. There is the tendency in our culture to blame every death on supernatural causes but I stand here today, and I am speaking not only as her sister, but also as a medical practitioner and a registered nurse. Let me be very clear. My sister died from complications with diabetes. The autopsy report clearly states that she went into a diabetic coma after being infused with glucose, which caused her blood sugar levels to be elevated, and it ultimately killed her. Was she killed? Yes, no doubt about that. Was it intentional? I don't believe so. Was it preventable? Yes. So instead of all the accusations and recriminations, what we should all be focusing on is what can be done to make sure that none of our children, mothers, fathers, brothers, and sisters die the way she died. And how can we prevent this from ever happening again? One word: education.

"I can say with all certainty that my sister would be alive today, if the nurse who attended to her was trained on recognizing diabetic symptoms. She would be alive today, if the nurse was trained to follow the proper procedure before rendering treatment. She would be alive today, if she herself knew the symptoms. So all of us need to be educated about this deadly disease. The education has to start from the highest levels, from the president to the government ministers being educated enough to provide adequate funding for the training of doctors, nurses, and all healthcare workers. Government must embark on a massive health campaign to educate the masses on this deadly but preventable and treatable disease.

In the United States alone, twenty-nine million people have diabetes. Twenty-one million of those have been diagnosed and most are living normal lives, thanks to a combination of awareness, education on how to manage it, and medication. Lives are being saved, because the United States government in partnership with private organizations that made it their business to curb the prevalence of this disease, which if left unchecked, could cripple their economy. If a country as advanced as the United States is worried about this disease, then we ought to be scared. According to the International Diabetes Federation, there are 567,300 diabetics in Cameroon. That is a staggering and sobering statistic (http://www.idf.org/membership/afr/cameroon) Think about the unreported numbers. Think about the people who dropped dead, seemingly without a cause. It is a scary thought, at least to me.

"My fellow countrymen and women, this is no joking matter. I know you didn't come to my sister's funeral to hear a lecture, but I strongly believe this is a lecture we all need to hear. It's a lecture we all need to understand and use that knowledge to put pressure on the government to take care of its responsibility for the health of its citizens. The message needs to be sent loud and clear to the President and the Minister of Public Health. And maybe, while we're at it, ask His Excellency the President and the honorable minister a simple question or two. How many times have they been treated at any of the general hospitals in this country? I am very positive that when our dear President and the honorable minister of public health travel the world, they visit hospitals. And I am sure they must have noticed that none of those look like the ones under their control. What are they doing to improve the appalling conditions of our hospitals? Maybe if we start demanding answers and holding our top officials accountable, things will start to change. Maybe that accountability will trickle down, and doctors will start answering to the sometimes egregious and negligent practices that lead to so many unnecessary deaths, causing untold hardships to innocent families.

"It is clearly evident that the government has been derelict in its duty to provide basic health care for all its citizens. While we put pressure on the government, we cannot sit back and wait for it to wake up from its slumber. We have to do our part. Let us draw on the spirit of cooperation that has united and enabled all of us to be here today, to mobilize and disseminate the information about diabetes. It is important for everyone to know what it is, recognize the symptoms, and more importantly, know how to manage it, so that no family experiences what my family and I are going through today.

"So just what is this killer disease? According to the US-based <u>National Institute of Diabetes and Digestive and Kidney Diseases</u>, diabetes is a complex group of diseases with a variety of causes. People with diabetes have high blood glucose, also called high blood sugar or hyperglycemia. It is a disorder of metabolism—the way the body uses digested food for energy. The digestive tract breaks down carbohydrates—sugars and starches found in many foods—into glucose, a form of sugar that enters the bloodstream. With the help of the hormone insulin, cells throughout the body absorb glucose and use it for energy. Diabetes develops when the body doesn't make enough insulin or is not able to use insulin effectively, or both. No one is certain what starts the processes that cause diabetes, but scientists believe genes and environmental factors interact to cause diabetes in most cases. There are two types of diabetes: type 1 and type 2. Type 2 diabetes—the most common form of diabetes—is caused by a combination of factors, including insulin resistance, a condition in which the body's muscle, fat, and liver cells do not use insulin effectively. Type 2 diabetes develops when the body can no longer produce enough insulin to compensate for the impaired ability to use insulin.

"Now that we know what diabetes is, how can we tell if we indeed have it? With the poor health-care system that we have, the lack of information about this disease is a major cause for concern. I suspect many people have this disease but don't know that they have it. In developed countries, people routinely get tested, and in addition to that, tests kits are easily available for people to test themselves. Since we are not privileged to have those services, there are simple warning signs and tests that all of us can use to determine if we are diabetic or not, namely:

1. Increased thirst

2. Increased frequency of urination

3. Increased frequency of lightheadedness or dizziness

4. Urinate in an open area and see if your urine foams a lot

5. Urinate in an open area and see if ants gather to feast on your urine

If the last two conditions of this self-tests are present, there is a very good chance that you are diabetic. At that point, go to the hospital, and make sure they do not infuse you with glucose or drip.

"So now that you have found out you are diabetic, how do you control it? Well, first of all, we are all different. Everybody's body is different and will react differently to the various remedies available. One of the first things to do is to control your diet. Diet is very critical to our overall health. Because our staples are all full of carbohydrates, try to limit the amount of food you eat at a time. Don't eat two bundles of fufu or achu at one go. Divide each bundle in two, and eat both within four hours of each other. A good rule of thumb is to eat small quantities of food every two hours. We are blessed with fresh vegetables. Eat lots of them.

"Exercise! Physical inactivity and obesity are strongly associated with the development of type 2 diabetes. Two generations ago, we were more active, walking everywhere we went. Our foods are all carbohydrates and have basically stayed the same. However, today, our lifestyles have changed. We live more sedentary lives, thus increasing our propensity to be obese. Obesity can be countered by exercise. Try to get at least thirty minutes of moderate-intensity physical activity five days a week. If you have not been active, start off slowly, building up to your strength. Try brisk walking, dancing, jogging, or any physical activity that helps get your heart rate up.

"If you are fat, try to lose weight. Losing weight by eating healthy and getting more physical activity not only can help you prevent diabetes, but it also lowers your risk for heart disease, certain types of cancer, arthritis, and many other health problems. Also, you will feel better and have more energy to do the things you enjoy.

"Last but not the least, take your medications regularly! The combination of all these things I have mentioned and your medicine will keep you relatively healthy and alive and minimize the risk of future complications. You will be able to live long enough to see your children and grandchildren.

"As I said before, diabetes is a deadly disease, and ignorance about it can be deadly. Complications from the lack of control or treatment can lead to blindness, heart diseases, amputations, and ultimately, death. We all must rethink our belief system, where every death is perceived and attributed to supernatural and superstitious causes. Diabetes, like any other disease that is left untreated, will kill you. You will drop dead, not because some distant uncle killed you and not because some witch doctor divined your fate, but because your ignorance about your health just killed you. I know we are all here to remember and celebrate my sister, and I am sorry for upstaging her death, but again, it is necessary so that we don't have to find ourselves in this situation, mourning another unnecessary death.

"My family and I will be forever indebted to you all for the love you have shown us. I personally want to thank the *benskineurs* for their incredibly unbridled show of support from the day my sister passed. Words cannot begin to describe the fact that not a single one of you are out there hustling and trying to make ends meet, just so all of you could honor my sister. Such a spirit of unity is unprecedented, and I think the wider communities should learn a thing or two from you. I urge you not to let that unitary spirit die, for if harnessed, it could be a formidable force for change, not only for you, but for your children and your children's children.

"In memory of my sister, I pledge to help educate as many people as possible about this disease through an organization that my family will start in her honor. The organization will be called: Forgoodnesssakes. The goal of the organization will not only be to disseminate information, but will also provide diabetic test kits to as many people as possible as a first line of defense against diabetes. If you would like to make a contribution toward this effort, please visit: www.forgoodnesssakes.org. If you have stories about diabetes that you would like to share, please write to mamasango2016@gmail.com. On behalf of my family, I thank you all for being here."

25

NURSE LOVELINE

Every single news outlet fawned over Mama Sango's funeral night and day, following the burial. Some rebroadcast Marie-Noel's speech over and over, providing commentary, dissecting, analyzing, and some injecting political satire. Critics and supporters clashed.

"Who does she think she is? I am sick of these *bushfallers* coming here and telling us what we should and should not be doing," commented a very harsh critic on a Sunday morning talk show, dismissively ignoring the thrust of the speech's message.

The entire Abakwa community held its breath in anticipation of the first broadcast of *Tori Time*, the radio show that brought the news of Mama Sango's demise to the community.

At about 3:45 p.m. on the Monday following Mama Sango's funeral, Marie-Noel rested comfortably on her sister's bed, so she could smell her and get closer to her. She held the pillows close to her bosom, burying her face into the fluffy light-brown surface.

"Auntie, some people are here to see you," her niece called out from the living room.

She wasn't expecting any guests, but this is home and guest didn't announce their visits, especially during this mourning period. She was lightly dressed in shorts and a light blue T-shirt. The two men standing at the entrance took notice of her shapely figure.

"Hello, Marie! Sorry for interrupting your sleep, and we are sorry for your loss. We really liked your speech the other day and were wondering if could talk to you about it."

Marie instantly remembered the passing conversation she had with the attendant at the hotel she was staying in. She had taken a liking to the soft-spoken, respectful, and ever-smiling attendant the first night she checked in. She always made it a point to stop and chat with her, inquiring about her future plans. "Some two men have been here looking for you," she had told Marie, before describing them.

Marie's heart beat faster, but she stayed calm. "Please, come in and have a seat," she invited them.

As the men proceeded to take their seats, they noticed through the open windows that a small crowd had formed around their car, and some more Ntamulung Junction residents were heading their way. "Sorry, we really have to go now. We will be back some other time."

Cars with no license plates were a telltale sign of the notoriously feared secret police. Someone had spotted the car in front of Pa Sango's house and alerted the neighborhood. In the past, there has been an instance of one of these cars being burnt by an angry mob, with the occupants narrowly escaping. As the two men entered the car to leave, one of the young men warned, "No come back again."

The jingle for *Tori Time* was barely finished when Akumbom Elvis Mc Carthy announced, "Contri pepo, tori we ih di enter for we tok tok house say mboma don show yi head for Ntamulung Junction for the one and only Mama Sango yi Ntang. Okada pepo dem, over to wuna." (Fellow countrymen, the much feared secret police have been spotted at Mama Sango's residence.)

Seven *benskineurs* showed up at Ntamulung Junction within five minutes of the announcement. Across town, many more were unloading their passengers and heading straight to Ntamulung Junction. Within hours, Ntamulung Junction teamed with *benskineurs*. In a hastily called meeting, plans were in place to maintain a round-the-clock presence around Pa Sango's residence, and three people were to accompany Marie-Noel wherever she went. Marie checked out of the hotel that night and called the United States embassy in Yaoundé to alert them of the situation. The *benskineurs* took it upon themselves to ensure her safety. She never spent another night in the same location twice again.

*   *   *

Marie-Noel was determined to set an example. She was going to file a lawsuit against the hospital, the attending doctor, and the nurse who *killed* her sister. Putting all the available paperwork together prior to the meeting with the lawyer, Marie-Noel had an urge to meet the nurse who treated her sister to hear about her sister's last moments. She wanted, once and for all, to find out exactly what transpired.

Unaware of the reasons for her visit and believing she was just another visitor, the nurse in charge guided Marie-Noel to see Nurse Loveline. The shock was immobilizing.

Marie recoiled at the sight of Nurse Loveline lying in bed, still hooked up to machines after the reconstructive surgery. On the day of her sister's death, Nurse Loveline had panicked after Mama Sango convulsed and was dying right before her eyes after the glucose infusion. In the confusion that ensued, she ran out of the clinic and straight into an oncoming *benskin*. The collision was hard, and Nurse Loveline landed facedown on the hard tarred surface, shattering all the bones on her face.

Marie-Noel knelt down, and wept.

ACKNOWLEDGMENTS

I would like to thank Uncle Peter Tayuka(rip), Sema Pefok, Elvis Edinge, Joice Zama, Lesline Folabit-Deffo, Vivian Ngang, Irene Zama, Fred Cham, Katie MacWilliams, Charles Zama, Dr. Stanley P. Ngeyi, Pastor Sambila Tamon, Mangie Susan Aleri Zama(rip), Akipus and Grace Fongu, Dr. Isaac Zama, Emmanuel and Isabelle Warah, Dr. Ivan Zama, Dr. Maggi Mekai-Vekima, and most especially, Queen Elizabeth Ndisang.

CPSIA information can be obtained at www.ICGtesting.com
Printed in the USA
LVOW10s1507210716

497248LV00016B/499/P